A Key to Treehouse Living is the adventure of William Tyce, a boy without parents, who grows up near a river in the rural Midwest. In a glossary-style list, he imparts his particular wisdom on subjects ranging from ASPHALT PATHS, BETTA FISH, and MULLET to MORTAL BETRAYAL, NIHILISM, and REVELATION. His improbable quest—to create a reference volume specific to his existence—takes him on a journey down the river by raft (see MYSTICAL VISION, see NAVIGATING BIG RIVERS BY NIGHT). He seeks to discover how his mother died (see ABSENCE) and find reasons for his father's disappearance (see UNCERTAINTY, see VANITY). But as he goes about defining his changing world, all kinds of extraordinary and wonderful things happen to him.

Unlocking an earnest, clear-eyed way of thinking that might change your own, *A Key to Treehouse Living* is a story about keeping your own record straight and living life by a different code.

A KEY TO TREEHOUSE LIVING

Published by Tin House Books, Portland, Oregon, and
Brooklyn, New York

Distributed by W. W. Norton & Company

Library of Congress Cataloging-in-Publication Data

Names: Reed, Elliot, author.
Title: A key to treehouse living / by Elliot Reed.
Description: First U.S. edition. | Portland, Oregon : Tin House
Books, 2018.
Identifiers: LCCN 2018024171 | ISBN 9781947793040
(hardcover)
Classification: LCC PS3618.E43556 K49 2018 | DDC
813/.6--dc23
LC record available at https://lccn.loc.gov/2018024171

First US Edition 2018
Printed in the USA
Interior design by Diane Chonette
www.tinhouse.com

A KEY TO TREEHOUSE LIVING

WITHDRAWN

ELLIOT REED

 TIN HOUSE BOOKS / Portland, Oregon & Brooklyn, New York

THIS BOOK IS FOR MY MOTHER,
KATHERINE REED

Now I am ready to tell how bodies are changed
Into different bodies.

From OVID'S METAMORPHOSIS, translated
by Ted Hughes (Chapter: *Creation; Four Ages;
Lycaon; Flood*)

ABSENCE

A woman becomes a mother when a baby comes out of her body. From then on, she can never stop being a mother. No matter how much or how little mothering she does, she will still be a mother. If a bird lays an egg in a nest, flies off, and never returns, the bird will still be a mother if the egg she laid hatches. Not all mothers want to be with their children.

ALPHABETICAL ORDER

An order for words to go in so that people can find what they're looking for without having to read every single one of the words. Generally, A comes before B and B before C and so on through Z, but sometimes it doesn't work exactly because whoever put the words in a list got distracted while writing down the words. Also, it may not work because sometimes a system may look like it's a good system for a while and then not seem like such a good system later. ADDITION may come before ABACUS, for instance, because you need to know what addition is before you can understand what an abacus does, and since you'd have to go and look up ADDITION if you ever looked up ABACUS, the sensible author would put ADDITION before ABACUS, and the sensible reader might as well read the whole list of words through, from start to finish.

ARCHAEOLOGY

If a man working as a landscaper for the city is digging a hole for a tree in a park, by himself, using a shovel, and as he throws a last shovelful of dirt onto the grass beside the hole sees a stone object fall out of a dirt clod, and when he picks it up sees that it's a spearpoint made a thousand years ago by a Native American, he becomes an archaeologist. Professional archaeologists like Indiana Jones or the guy from Jurassic Park get paid to look for ancient artifacts and then to say some things about what they find, to say what the thing they found tells us about the past. Amateur archaeologists—like the city-park worker who finds the spearpoint or a kid who finds a black-and-white photograph of his father stashed beneath a dust-covered chest of drawers in his uncle's basement while searching beneath it for a Matchbox car that took its ramp badly and disappeared down there—don't get paid to look for artifacts and don't have to, if they don't want to, say anything to anyone about what they find (see BUS, STOPPED).

AFTER THE FACT
Too late. If somebody who was here a moment ago is now gone, and you didn't see them leave, you've found out they're gone after the fact—the fact being that they left.

ASPHALT PATH
The park on 78th is a standard city park including one undersized baseball field with bleachers and dugouts, a locking shed, rubber bases in good condition, and a digital scoreboard. An overgrown asphalt path goes around the outfield. The path is shaded by sycamore and fir trees, many of which have large, dead limbs. Go to the big park downtown and you won't find dead limbs threatening from the trees. In that park, crews of beige-uniformed park workers go from tree to tree in beat-up pickups maintaining the wood. The park on 78th, while soundly within the radius of municipal park maintenance, is cared for by the parents of young baseball players, along with two elderly women who wander the weedy outfield picking dandelion greens. I once saw a grown man in a camouflage coat and boots without shoelaces ride a kid's bike down the asphalt path, slowly, as if he were lost, holding a

plastic-wrapped bouquet of roses in one hand and steering the bike with the other.

ANGER, JEALOUS

If you want something and can't have it, and then you see other people getting the thing you can't have, you will probably feel jealousy. Lots of times, though, jealousy is a short-lived feeling that quickly becomes anger. Jealousy, in its purest form, is observable at your local Little League game. See the kid straddling a stopped bike out past the outfield, the kid staring at the game and oblivious to everything else? There you see jealousy. If he holds in his hand a small branch, and if he breaks this branch on the trunk of a fir tree as he bikes away from the ball field, you've seen jealous anger, but a harmless kind. Then there are other kinds of jealous anger.

ANNOTATIONS

It's important that you have a reference book to refer to in case you get confused. If you don't have one, find one, and remember: not all reference books are created equal. Some are more useful than others. If you find that your reference book contains bad information, you must fix it by making special corrections called annotations—use pen, pencil, or crayon to correct what's wrong so the next person who reads it knows better. Alberta Otter's reference book was an old dictionary printed by LITTLE AND IVES in 1828, which Alberta got in 1910 and had until 1925, which I know because she dated her annotations. She went through the whole LITTLE AND IVES dictionary, annotating front to back, which I know because the dates on the annotations go up as the letters go toward Z. In 1925, while annotating XYLOPHONE, Alberta abandoned her dictionary in a hurry. I believe she abandoned her dictionary because her family's middle-of-nowhere Victorian was being attacked by bandits from Kansas. It looked like a bandit had searched the dictionary for money and then dropped it, open, on the floor of an upstairs bedroom, which is where I found it in the old Victorian that had become an overgrown ruin in the park downtown. A family of mice had moved into the pages of the dictionary and was living in the entries. Most of the dictionary had been tunneled out by the time I found it, but there was still enough of it left. The dictionary was splayed face-down on the floor, open to page 1094. What I found on page 1094 was a printed sketch of a raccoon beneath the entry entitled RACCOON, but you only realized that the creature in the sketch was supposed to be a raccoon because it had its name right there. Beside the printed sketch were Alberta's annotations in cursive: BOBCAT? BEAR? which I understood to be her agreeing with what I was thinking, agreeing with me through this dictionary across time, agreeing that whoever had been told to sketch a raccoon for LITTLE AND IVES had never actually seen one. Alberta's annotated dictionary has notes that the mice didn't eat on 201 of the 2,000 pages, notes as short as one word and other notes as long as a page. The word ANNOTATIONS, written in Alberta's cursive, has six ink humps. Alberta sometimes gave the humps of her cursive M's and N's little beards of snow, which is how I can tell that she missed seeing the mountains.

ATHABASCAN

This is the language of Eskimos. If you look up ATHABASCAN in Alberta's dictionary, you will learn that there are many ways to say SNOW in Athabascan. You will also learn that the Athabascan language is almost a dead language, meaning Eskimos are switching to English and are forgetting all their old words. Countless languages have been born and have died. Languages are born and die every day, and it keeps getting harder and harder to keep your language alive. The good news is you can hear Athabascan after it's gone because the library has recordings of Eskimos telling stories in their igloos.

BAD DOG

It's hard to say if any given dog is totally bad or totally good. It's possible that no dog is either. Still, it's a good idea to at least consider that a dog that comes at you after you've climbed a fence with a sign on it that reads BAD DOG may behave badly toward you. Dogs can do bad things and good things, and it's easier to run across a dog that's engaged in bad behavior than one doing good. A bad dog in somebody's house might earn its badness by eating cat poop from the cat's litter box, eating the cat itself, tearing up the furniture, or peeing in the laundry. A good dog might bring in the newspaper. If you're trying to sneak into an abandoned, vine-covered Victorian in the park, and you and your buddy Ned climb over a fence that surrounds the house, and the fence is hung with a sign that reads BAD DOG—let's say you and your pal are doing it in the name of archaeology—and when you get over you see an overweight poodle snoozing in the shade of a tree, you must assume that this dog, no matter how harmless or cuddly it looks, is a bad dog. Proceed quietly past the poodle and into the house.

BREEDING DOGS

Most dogs are mutts, which means that their parents were two different kinds of dogs—that no human was around to breed them. This is along the same lines as good and bad dogs—no dog is outright one or the other by nature. There are no naturally purebred cocker spaniels out there because a dog naturally likes to leave his family and explore the woods alone, to explore and find different-looking dogs to hump. The point is, if you want a purebred cocker spaniel, you have to visit a dog breeder and pick one out from the spaniel pack that lives in his dog cage. The dog breeder lives off the main road and he keeps his cage out of sight. Most of the time the dogs in the cage have good manners, but not always. If one of them acts up, he gets sequestered in a cage of his own where he must think about what he has done. A serious dog breeder will need a part-time helper to clean out the cages and wash the dogs before somebody arrives to buy one of them. If a dog breeder offers you a job helping out on weekend mornings for four bucks an hour, do it, but don't expect to do it for very long. When a dog breeder hires a ten-year-old kid to do a job, he knows it's a temporary thing. He doesn't expect that kid to be working in the cages when he turns eleven. Most dogs would rather be outside a cage than inside one no matter how old they are, especially when you're in there trying to clean, and it's bad to be in a cage full of dogs that don't want you in their cage. On top of all that, you'll lock eyes, on accident, with a puppy who wants to bond with you, and since puppies are just about the best there is at bonding, he will bond you to him and you will spend the whole time thinking about how to spring him and you'll neglect your duties and the breeder will threaten to fire you, and the dogs will all start barking at once, and the breeder will kick the very puppy you're bonding with—not roughly, but enough to make the puppy yelp—and you'll have to grit your teeth, spit on the ground if you need to, but you'll have to keep on scrubbing the turds off the floor of the cage. You'll wash another five cocker spaniels and then, after the breeder has paid you, you'll come back at night and claim your puppy. A purebred cocker spaniel goes for a hundred bucks, but one that's been abused should go for much less, and so your day's earnings will have to suffice, or maybe just half your day's earnings—twelve dollars—which is good money any way you look at it. Leave the cash in the cage and go, only do so without setting all the dogs off. This will entail your purchasing a six-pack of pork steaks from the country gas station down the road from the breeder and taking another three from your uncle's mansion, further cutting into your day's earnings, but it will be worth it. Running down a gravel road in the moonlight with a new dog by your side makes a pretty good feeling.

BALLOONS

Some years back, when the Midway Raptors were still dominating kid-pitch Little League, a trio of specialized weather balloons came floating over the ballpark in the arms of a gale that had come through downtown ahead of a storm. This was the middle of spring, on a day when El Hondero had chosen to bring out the balloons and make sure their sensors were working. I hadn't met him yet but I saw what happened with his balloons, and later he told me about the causes of the accident. He'd only been working for the Department of Air Quality for a month and he hated the job. The only way you could get away from the Air Quality office was if you went out and calibrated the balloons. El Hondero would later say he had not been in a sound state of mind, having just gone through the end of a romance, and that this led him to drink alcohol and then make the decision to fly the balloons after making sure the Air Quality sensors were working. He says he never noticed the massive black storm clouds, which is understandable, since in springtime the storm clouds often come in the middle of a sunny day only to disappear again within the space of half an hour. That day, a gale came up and ripped the balloons away from El Hondero, who began to pursue them on foot. The balloons carried a lot of expensive science instruments and were never meant to be released in heavy weather. The storm took the balloons across downtown and over the park on 78th, where the Raptors were winning 15–2 in the bottom of the sixth. I saw the balloons from where I stood, past the outfield, straddling my bicycle, hoping somebody would quit or get hurt so I could play. Then the game stopped so everyone could watch the balloons float by. I remember how strange it was that the balloons were so huge and so silent. Then one of the balloons began to deflate as it passed over the ballpark, making a hissing sound and coming to a landing on a car that had stopped at an intersection. A minute later the sky went black and it began to pour rain. The motorist beneath the wrecked balloon emerged dry but frazzled when the rain-soaked Little Leaguers peeled it away from her car. The other balloons continued on their way, one getting caught up in power lines a block away and the other driven into a sycamore tree after a flight of almost a mile. This was the last time El Hondero flew balloons.

BALLOON DOGGIE

Statue of a dog made of a long, slim balloon blown up and twisted by a clown. At one time, a clown was forced to use his big red lips if he wanted to blow up his long, tight balloons, but nowadays he uses a hand pump. How you get a balloon doggie is you go to a party where a clown is working or you go to a fair and find one there. He'll offer you the option of a doggie or a giraffe, which is just a dog with a long neck in the eyes of a clown, and he'll let you choose its color. It's always fun to watch him twist his balloons for you, and it's almost always fun to get the doggie in the end, but there are times when the appearance of a balloon doggie in your life will not be such a happy thing, and I'm not talking about those times when you get a balloon doggie and find yourself fixated on its future, deflated state. I'm talking about when your uncle steals your cocker spaniel and puts a balloon doggie in its place.

BEANS, JELLY

Each April, on a Sunday, is a day they call Easter. On this day the custom is for adults to distribute edible and inedible plastic eggs across the land. Some adults will also spread jelly beans. Later, children will romp forth in search of the hidden treasures. Easter was originally established to celebrate the reanimation of a martyred guru and his subsequent ascension into heaven, though this boring myth has been replaced with the more exciting one of a live, talking rabbit who is said to be hiding the plastic eggs and jelly beans.

BETTA FISH

A type of fish that comes in many colors and likes more than anything to fight other Betta Fish. Betta Fish are the gladiators of the fish world. If you choose to have a Betta Fish for a pet, be sure to put only one Betta Fish in a fish tank. If you put more than one Betta Fish in a tank they will fight, and the fight will end with only one Betta Fish left alive. People like Betta Fish because they have beautiful fins that flow like silk and because they are easy to take care of as long as you keep them from fighting too much. Betta Fish are more reliable than grown-up men because you can be sure that two Betta Fish will fight when you put them together but you can never be sure with men. Betta Fish can cure you of nightmares if you hold them in your mouth for ten seconds each night before you go to sleep. Fill your mouth with water from the tap, lean your head back and open your mouth, then drop in the fish. Close your mouth and let him dust his fins on the insides of your cheek. This relationship is like the one between remora and shark. By cleaning your cheeks, the fish is absorbing your nightmares. The darker the Betta Fish, the more nightmares it has absorbed, and once it is black it cannot absorb any more nightmares, so you will want to pick out a light-colored Betta Fish if your plan is to use it as a cure for bad dreams. See DREAMS OF THE BETTA FISH for some potential side effects of using a fish to stave off bad dreams.

BUOYANCY
What you have that makes you float. Does what the word sounds like it does with its B and its U bobbing up.

Memories have buoyancy. They bob up to the surface like corks. My parents and I lived in a bus until my mom went away and my dad and I moved out of the bus for some reason. That's when we moved in with my uncle. I say we, but mostly it was me. My dad moved in, and then he moved out. You can put all your clothes and your toothbrush in a bag but not be moving anywhere—you can just be going. Whether it's moving is up to you. If two grown men get in a fight, it's not a fight like at school. They will yell and knock things over and it will all happen really quickly. It will come out of nowhere and they'll say they're sorry afterward. But if one of the men puts his clothes and his toothbrush in a bag and says he's going on a trip, you can be sure that what he's actually doing is moving away, but you'll only realize it later (see AFTER THE FACT).

I remember my uncle floating in the pond on an inner tube, spinning slowly on the water, playing the bugle for me. His eyebrows and moustache were wet and dripping, and he was squinting, bugling, making his eyebrows dance, hoping I would laugh. I remember being drawn to the water but afraid of it, and being afraid of my uncle. I remember running up the dock to where my dad was lying in the grass and I remember him taking me and hugging me, then getting up and walking away. Until another memory comes bobbing up, that's the last of him I have—that's the day he disappeared for good and left me with my uncle. What's most buoyant about that memory is the feeling of my dad's shirt. It was warm and soft, but crisp in its wrinkles where my face was pressed to it. What I don't remember is the color of the shirt, where he was going, why I didn't go with him, or what he said to me when he left. Judging by the buoyancy of memory, the sensation of his shirt was more important.

BEEF IN BED

While nothing really helps the physical pain of eighteen beestings, an ice pack and a hamburger will make you feel better about the fact that you got stung. Bees don't sting cows, is what you could tell yourself is the reason, because cows have no business in the woods that would cause them to go stomping on rotten logs beneath sycamore trees. The real reason why beef helps beestings is that it feels good to have your uncle bring you a burger in bed for the first time in all the years you've lived with him. Seeing him come in with a plate for you will cancel out the pain.

BEFITTING

When something makes sense given the circumstances. If you get stung by a bunch of bees, do this: show your uncle the welts, lie down on your bed, and wait for him to bring you an ice pack and a hamburger. Put the ice on your head and slowly eat the burger. Concentrate on the taste of the food and the cold of the ice on your head, and then share some burger with your Betta Fish. Break the beef up into little bits so he can fit them in his mouth. If he's a good fighter, he will suck the beef into his mouth, swim in a circle, spit the beef out, and repeat. It is befitting if, for example, you are sitting on your bed, stung-up by bees and eating a burger, watching your Betta Fish eat his, and your uncle comes in to see how you're feeling, looks at what's happening in the tank, and says, "Fighting fish is beefing up, I see." After your uncle leaves you hop off the bed and grab Alberta's dictionary and look up BEEFING UP and find it buried in the entry titled BEEF and then right there below BEEF you see the word BEFITTING—there's a moment you could call befitting.

BOOMS
Thunder, The Rolling Rumbler, is a sound associated with shivering leaves, rippling bodies of water, fast-moving gray clouds, starlessness, lightning, and the galloping of horses from open prairies to the shelter of trees. Birds love to wing madly in thunder-filled spring-time air, disappearing just an instant before the deluge of rain that most often runs with the Rumbler. The Rumbler loves nothing more than to show up for Easter

Sunday. Men, women, children, and horses have all been vaporized by lightning while in the act of eating jelly beans in fields on Easter.

BLACK ASH

When an object is struck by lightning, a nuclear shock wave, or a sound of tremendous magnitude, that object will become vaporized. There are three types of vaporization: Partial, Total, and Subliminal. Partially vaporized objects become piles of black, reflective ash. Totally vaporized objects become puffs of smoke, and merge with the wind so quickly that no one has ever seen it actually happen. If you're a baby and your parents set you down for a minute to go hide jelly beans in a field on Easter but then they get totally vaporized by lightning, you'll have to go live with your uncle.

BOMBED OUT or SUBLIMINAL VAPORIZATION

If an object has been struck by lightning but has been neither partially nor totally vaporized, that is to say the object still appears to be the thing that it is, then the object has been subliminally vaporized. The inner energy of the object converts into a warm, invisible haze that rises into the atmosphere, never to return to its one-time host. A horse, for example, may be subliminally vaporized and still try to approach you when you hold out a carrot, though the way she looks at you will betray the fact that there's nothing going on in there—you could knock on the door but nobody would be home.

BABY NO LONGER A BABY

At some point, a baby stops being a baby. One idea is that a baby is less a baby with each new word it utters, and that it finally stops being a baby when it realizes it can say what it wants to say without having to start crying. When a baby points at something and makes a sound, it thinks the sound it has made represents that thing. No matter if the baby points at a lawn mower and says RACE CAR or if he actually points to a car when he says it, nearby adults will encourage him by smiling at him and making baby sounds of their own or by tickling his little baby feet. A baby's desire to make words gets stronger when people encourage him, but so does his desire to speak correctly, to give something the COR-RECT name, that is, whatever name gets the most adults smiling and nodding. I once knew a kid who still had a lot of his baby language. He called grass "skin" and rotting wood "slug" and I don't remember much else but it was a really good language and I sometimes wonder if his language is still alive somewhere, but I don't hold out much hope.

BABY MEMORIES

Everybody wishes they had more baby memories, because back then it was all a vacation and everything was a game and all you needed was air and milk and we've forgotten what that felt like. Sadly, baby memories don't exist. One theory about babies says that the moment a baby realizes it has a memory is the moment it becomes a child. If you can take something you're experiencing and know that you're going to remember it later, then you are not a baby anymore. What you remember as your earliest memory is the end of you as a baby. A memory that feels like your earliest can come to you out of the blue (see KERNELS OF THE PAST), and so your childhood can expand or contract. My earliest memory came to me out of the blue one day while I was playing a game with my uncle in the basement of his mansion, where I lived at the time, and when I had it I instantly became older.

BREEZE, BLUSTERY

Wind is the world's greatest traveler. Wind moves the fastest of all things, and it makes the greatest journeys, traveling as far as the sun and back. Wind spends a lot of time running ahead of big thunderstorms, bouncing around in the graying sunlight, shivering tree leaves, conscripting anything light and airy as it races across the earth. A breeze is a gust of wind, and days that are breezy are called blustery. Everything is influenced by the weather. It's more common to meet strangers on blustery days than it is to meet them on calm ones. People get blown in like leaves fallen from faraway trees. On blustery days, light objects being blown across the ground are said to be skittering. Fly balls sail in curves. Ned was chasing a pop fly when a gust of wind curved its path and brought it out to me where I stood past the fence. He asked me for it and I threw it to him, but I took a while to throw it because I liked the feel of the ball in my hand. Then everyone was yelling at Ned to throw it in. They blamed Ned for what was done by the wind. I told Ned his team was better off without him and said I needed help building a treehouse.

BRIGHTNESS OF SUNLIGHT

Anytime you're awake and outside in the daytime, no matter what it is you're looking at, you're seeing sunlight bouncing off the thing that you're seeing. If you look at your hand and see skin, that's actually sunlight reflecting off of what you have come to know as your skin. When a storm cloud rolls through and it's daytime, let's say it's Easter because storms happen a lot around then, if a thundercloud covers up all the sky you can see, everything turns a little bit gray. Even bright colors get some gray in them. So let's say, for example, a child discovers a jelly bean beneath a wet log rotting in the pasture behind his uncle's mansion. He hears thunder. He sees the horses watching him from the cover of a stand of cedars, and he hears someone calling to him to come inside but he doesn't go because he's seen this jelly bean, which could be red but is also gray, and he wonders what to name the color. Unless he realizes that everything around him is a reflection of sunlight, which in this moment is gray because a storm has rolled in, he will be vaporized by lightning. It would be stupid to die while wondering about the color of a jelly bean. A final thing about brightness and its use in the nighttime: my uncle once told me that things are the same whether or not there's light shining on them. He taught me about how if you're alone in your room and it's dark out and you start to see things grow and transform in the darkness of your room, just picture the way your room looks when sunlight is shining in through the window. You won't be scared anymore, and the next thing you know it'll be morning.

BUGLING

There are many different brass instruments known to man, one of which is the bugle. Before you start bugling, make sure that what you have is actually a bugle. Bugles can be recognized by their brass curves and lack of buttons. It is important that your bugle have a mouth-piece. That's the cone-shaped silver thing you blow the air into. Next you need to practice blowing correctly. Put your lips together and make a fart-like buzzing noise by pushing air through your tightly closed lips. The buzzing noise should not be made with air you have stored in the pocket of your mouth but rather with air from your lungs. Put your lips to the bugle and buzz into it. The buzzing sound is what creates bugle music. The bugle can be used to create a huge variety of sounds, and there are many different songs you can play once you get to be a good bugler. Even if you can't play any songs, you can still use the bugle to get the attention of someone in the distance.

BUGLING UNCLE
Look out across the shiny new mansions at the edge of town, at the nearly identical mansions built on huge lawns that butt up against the old forest, and imagine the kinds of people who live in these buildings. Odds are that one of them is somebody's uncle. My uncle made his fortune playing the bugle at nursing homes and then wisely investing his earnings in the stock market. "Remember this," he said one day when a teacher from my school called to talk to him on the phone about me, "remember this when people come up and tell you that something you're doing will never get you anywhere.

Remember about the time when your uncle got a five-dollar bill as a tip at a bugle gig, and how he decided on a whim to take it down to some hobos who hung out by the railroad tracks. He loved money, and he needed it, but for some reason on that one day he just knew he had to take the money down to the guys at the railroad tracks. Remember how one of those hobos turned out to be in real estate." I've never forgotten the story. He slammed the phone on its receiver, got down on one knee, and squeezed my hand tightly while he told it to me. I didn't know what REAL ESTATE meant, but I knew that it was good. My uncle said he was mostly retired by the time I moved in with him but he still blew the bugle once in a while and he'd never stopped thinking about money. I loved to run full-tilt through the long, carpeted halls of his mansion and down the stairs to the maze-like concrete basement. I'd run barefoot in the hot summer across the cool basement floor to the chest freezer stocked with plastic tubes of sweet, colored ice. My uncle never cared how many I had until one day when I melted some of the ice tubes and used the colored liquid for art, and then he stopped buying them.

BUS, STOPPED
If you're traveling through the countryside and you look off the road, you'll see a lot of stopped buses. If you look

carefully, sometimes you'll see people living in these buses. People live in buses the same way some kids live in treehouses and some gypsies live in parachutes (see GYPSY PARACHUTE HOUSE). I have a photograph I found on an archaeological expedition that proves I once lived in a stopped bus. The bus in the picture was once a school bus. Then my parents got it, drove it to the top of a hill, and shut off the engine for good. There's a table outside the folding door of the bus. There are plastic chairs around the table and an umbrella in the middle. Flowerpots hang from the bus's windows and there are two chaise lounges on the roof for watching the stars. My parents planted a garden right next to the bus and sat at the table in the shade of the umbrella after they worked in the garden. You see it all in the picture. Inside the bus, where you can't see, where there used to be seats for schoolchildren, there was a bed, a radio, and a bookcase. You can't see inside the bus in the picture but I remember what it was like because I've been in there myself. The baby in the photo is me. I'm on a blanket spread out in the garden and I'm tiny. My mother is there next to me, and my father is taking the picture. I know this because he wrote on the back of it, and because he printed the photo on the enlarger that my uncle kept hidden away in the basement.

BOREDOM

If it's pouring rain out and you're trapped inside for whole afternoons at a time, you'll have to come up with some way of entertaining yourself indoors, otherwise you will suffer from boredom. If you're used to being outside every afternoon—let's say you've gotten into a routine of exploring the woods around your treehouse, hacking paths through thickets and constructing elaborate booby traps for unwanted visitors, and let's say that you have a particularly elaborate booby trap in the works, a trap that is nearly complete and that must be completed soon because a gang of bullies has discovered the secret location of your tree fort—but it's pouring rain outside and so travel to the fort, much less construction of the booby trap, is not feasible, you will find yourself staring out the window at the dark clouds behind the tree line, dark and only getting darker, and you'll make bets on which drops of rain will be the first to make it down to the bottom of the windowpane: that's boredom. If you're lucky, you'll have a Betta Fish. A Betta Fish can be counted on to provide a solid hour or so of entertainment when presented with a photograph of another Betta Fish through the glass of its tank. There are only so many times a Betta Fish can attack the picture through the glass, though. If you give the fish the picture too often, you can hurt it. Boredom is not just dangerous for Betta Fish.

Boredom is also dangerous for your relationship with your uncle.

You get a lot of ideas when you're bored so it's important to tell the difference between a good idea and a bad idea. It's a bad idea, for instance, to melt ice pops on old photographic equipment. It's a good idea, on the other hand, to read a book. If you get bored of reading, you can write your own story or draw your own picture. But even that can get boring. I remember one particularly rainy spring when my uncle was always gone and I had whole days to myself. At the time, I was working on the best treehouse I'd ever built. The sycamore it was in was ancient and had perfect structure. The fort was surrounded by booby traps and had two little windows you could shoot rocks out of. Six kids once tried to take us over. They made it through the first line of booby traps and it was just me and Ned up there, but we were ready. Two versus six and we won. Ned sustained a stone to the eye thrown by a long-armed boy named Tony who, it turned out, was the top pitcher in Little League, but Ned didn't bleed for long and we were able to do far worse to the attackers. See—it's hard to write about boredom without getting distracted by telling something interesting. It was a high-caliber treehouse I had the year it was so rainy the pond tripled in size and sucked in one of the mansions being built on the other side of the pond, the year my uncle was always away at the tracks and I had so much time by myself that my imagination was too weak to defend me from boredom. My uncle was gone most of the time, and when he was home he was depressed because the bets weren't going his way. He would just watch the rain in silence and ignore me, and that's about the only time I ever wished I'd had another uncle or my original parents (see also NEGLECT). I tried, in desperation, to make it to the treehouse, which I knew must have been rotting in the torrential rain, but I ended up almost getting swept away by a stream that was deeper than I thought it was.

BOATING IN BASEMENTS

If your basement is flooded, you'll want to launch a boat. It will be impossible to get a canoe down the stairs, and an inner tube won't work because you won't want to touch the dirty water. The best thing to do when water fills your basement is to build a little boat and launch it into the flood. I used to spend hours launching little homemade boats on the staircase that disappeared into the water. In the basement was a dark, quiet sea that my uncle ignored. I remember floating candles, launching them on little boats on the sea in the basement and watching them burn out in the darkness—but even that became boring. I started talking to my Betta Fish. The fish became so bored that he began to swim upside down, so I cut him loose in the flood. And then, finally, I became so bored that I tried to read the phone book. I'd exhausted every book in the house by that point except one—a huge, ancient tome with a name so boring it actually gave me physical pain: FLYNN'S GUIDE TO WOODY TREES AND SHRUBS, EIGHTH EDITION. WITH ADDITIONAL FLOWCHARTS AND EXPANDED GLOSSARY. I found it beneath the kitchen sink and dragged it up to my room. On the cover was a faded black-and-white photograph of an expressionless man, dressed in an unremarkable shirt and unremarkable pants, standing beside a tree. I felt a glimmer of hope that this man might tell me, somewhere in this manual, something that I might be able to use to improve my tree fort. The pages were like a phone book and the print was almost as small. Most of the book seemed to be in Latin. The descriptions, when in English, were full of words I'd never heard before. For instance I kept running into the words WEEPING HABIT used in reference to certain Latin names. When at last I flipped to the back of the enormous book and found WEEPING HABIT in the glossary, I forgot ever to turn back. I was on my tenth reading of Flynn's glossary and had begun my first little list, a short catalog of all the things in my treehouse with entries like THROWING ROCK and ESCAPE ROPE and SPIRIT BEETLE when I realized that the boredom had receded.

CALIBRATING THE BALLOONS

Depending on what kind of gas you use to inflate a balloon and how big you inflate it, different things will happen when you let the balloon go. Inflating a balloon is one thing, though, and calibrating an inflated balloon is another. If you say you're going to calibrate a balloon, you mean you're working on a special weather-device the balloon carries with it when it floats into the sky. If on a windy spring day you are walking to the city park with your buddy Ned, who is on a skateboard, and if you choose to walk down a street full of vendors of hot foods, inevitably you will pass alleys. If you remember to always look down these alleys, or if your timing is perfect and he's just coming out of the alley and preparing to cross the busy street, you will have an encounter with the former Air Quality officer known as El Hondero. El Hondero will explain to you that he's been spending much of his time this spring exploring the shadowy alleys of downtown, walking and thinking, trying to make discoveries. You can't be sure what El Hondero is looking for in these alleys unless you ask him. One day he'll say he's looking for a lost cat that belongs to a friend, the next day he's recycling circuits behind the computer-repair shop. He almost always wears a beige-colored trench coat without a single hole or stain, no matter the weather, and the wiry black strands of his hair spill out across the shoulders despite his frequent attempts to tuck the strands behind his ears. It might be hard to guess based on the hair and the thick beard that sometimes covers his face, but El Hondero is a recent college graduate. El Hondero got fired for a number of reasons, but especially because of the accident, and he was forced to pay a lot of money to replace the specialized instruments. Since then he's abandoned his material connections to society so he can focus full-time on his archaeological research.

CLIMBING TREES

First make sure the tree isn't dead on the inside. Some trees can look alive but are actually totally rotted out. A good heavy kick to the trunk will help you figure out if it's rotten or not. If it sounds hollow or if your boot actually goes into the tree or if the tree falls down when you kick it then you know the tree is no good for climbing. Next make sure to check the canopy. That's the part of the tree above your head. If someone's already up there you will have to ask them for permission to climb, unless the tree is in fact your tree, in which case you will then have to decide whether to climb up there and join the other climber or whether you'll ask that climber to get out of your tree first.

CHOICES OF LOCOMOTION

How you get somewhere depends on when you have to be there and what the land is like between you and that place. In my dreams I get everywhere by zip line or by zeppelin or by flying. If there's a river, I canoe it. When I went to the moon in a dream and wrote a book about the different types of rocks there, I traveled with a rocket pack. In the real world, the options are more limited. If you have all day to get there, it's best to walk through the woods. The woods are better than the road because people aren't always trying to run you over or stop and pick you up. In the woods you can be left alone. If you come upon a tent in the woods and some clothes hanging from the branches of a tree nearby, don't go knock on the tent. The tent-camper in the woods within city limits is the kind of person who wants to be left alone. If he were in a treehouse it would be different, but the fact is the fun's long gone out of camping for him and he's sleeping close to the dirt because that's where he feels the safest.

CORK RAFT

Raft made of wine cork, toothpick, and napkin sail. Get a wine cork, stab a toothpick into it, and tape a triangular piece of cut-up napkin on the toothpick mast. Load it with passengers and let it go. The cork raft does well in a creek or a flooded basement. Its sail is mostly for show.

It'll still float if it tips. Put an ant on the cork raft and he'll stay on the cork even if it rolls totally over. Load him on using a second toothpick you've gotten him to climb onto. Don't expect to get a cork raft back after you've launched it. If you're too lazy to build one yourself, go down to the creek that runs through the park and check among the driftwood and stones. You'll find a lot of wine corks that were never cork rafts, and some whose masts have long since rotted away.

CAREFUL ENTRY OF NEGLECTED FORTS

If a fort has not been used for a while, like after the most rainy spring you can remember, odds are a snake or two will try it out. Often these are green tree snakes since, of course, forts are often found in trees. Most snakes are harmless, though some city parks are home to exotic venomous species that were kept as pets for a while and then released. A snake in a fort is best evicted with a long stick. If your fort is the type accessed from below with a trapdoor system, it's best to poke a mirror up through the trapdoor before you stick your head in so you can check for snakes from a position of safety.

CAUTION IN FORTS

Visitors usually appear in springtime. This is because people are spending more time outside once the weather

has turned nice, and inevitably they come across the tree
forts built in city parks over the winter—tree forts built
by crews of hardworking boys and girls who take breaks
to warm their hands over barrel fires after hammering
for hours in the frigid building season, some even traveling to and from the construction site on ice skates. In
the spring is when I'd be up in the fort with my pals and
we'd get visitors. Of course, we were prepared for visitors
of any nature: we were armed to the teeth but also had a
huge chestful of magazines, cards for playing and cards
for trading, cigarettes, fireworks, jelly beans, and a radio.
One time my uncle visited and took us all out to his mansion for Pop-Tarts and sodas. Another time, someone
claiming to be a fireman tried to come rescue us from our
perfectly comfortable tree fort. We had to beat on his
fingers with a hammer.

COURAGE

Courage is doing something risky. Sometimes, just getting out of bed in the morning requires courage. Other
times, you'll find yourself working up the courage to do
something risky and terrifying like jumping from a high
place into a body of water. You'll know you're "working
up the courage" when you look down and feel your body
talking to you—like when you're at the top of the cliff
and the lake looks like it's a mile below you, and there's

your pal Ned treading water in the expanding ripple from his cannonball and you feel your calves quiver, and what they're saying to you in calf language is "don't you dare," and they're probably right, you probably shouldn't. Or, take another example, an example where courage can lead to more substantial and long-lasting gains than the momentary thrill of falling through nothingness: a half mile or so from your uncle's mansion, where you're living, is a run-down trailer. You don't know the people who live in that trailer, but they look like they have an interesting take on life that might be different from the one you're used to, and, more importantly, it looks like they really know how to have a good time. So one day you decide to go up there and talk to them. You go up there and knock on the door, which is a screen door, and behind which is darkness, darkness and the sound of a little radio playing fuzzy country music, and you call out HELLO into the darkness and knock again, and this time you hear something thumping in the darkness, thumps followed by a crash, and, instinctively, you run. Courage, in this situation, would be to return to the trailer and bang on the door once more. Courage would be asking yourself, "What's the worst that could happen?" and not thinking for too long about the answer to that question.

CLEANING LADY

Cleaning ladies are mostly ladies, though there are one or two boys who have done it, but still the boss of the cleaning ladies, along with the people who have their mansions cleaned, call the cleaning ladies LADIES, even if one of those cleaning ladies is a boy. I know this because I was once a cleaning lady for a day. A teenager named Carla got me the job and I only lasted one day at it because it was the worst job I'd ever had and the pay was no good. Carla said they were desperate and since she kind of knew me I could join the crew. She said they'd hired a twelve-year-old before so thirteen was no big deal. I was on my way to the treehouse when Carla whistled at me from the front porch of her house. I stopped to see why she'd whistled and she told me the deal and said that work would start on Saturday. Tomorrow was Saturday, and Carla said that the boss would pay in cash and that one day's work could get me as much as fifty bucks. Fifty bucks would be enough to buy a camouflage parachute I'd had my eye on so I said yes to the job. This was sometime after the flood, a little before the gypsies came. Cleaning houses was a bad job right off the bat. First, Carla was thirty minutes late to pick me up. When she showed up she was in a truck being driven by her friend, another cleaning lady named Liz. Liz was so fat I could barely squeeze between her and Carla in the truck, and Liz was mean. Liz had a bottle of schnapps and was drinking it that morning and saying that whatever Carla said was stupid. Carla talked to Liz about me like I wasn't there. She told Liz that I was probably going to an orphanage and that my friend Ned had told her I wasn't like other kids. "You just tell this kid to do something and he'll get into it, whatever it is," she said, and Liz looked over at me for a second but then looked back at the road and took another sip of schnapps, which smelled a lot like a cleaning product. I could think of plenty of things I wouldn't do whether or not you told me to do it—drink that schnapps, for instance—but I didn't say anything because I could tell I wasn't supposed to talk and I could tell that it didn't really matter what anybody said. My feet got cold because the heat in the truck didn't work and I'd stepped in a puddle when I was getting in the car. Carla remembered she'd forgotten the vacuum so we had to go get it from her house. Liz called Carla a bunch of bad names on the way there and Carla didn't say anything back. She just smoked a cigarette and turned up the radio. Then Liz looked at a tree on the side of the road and called the tree a bad name, and that's when I realized bad names were most of the words that Liz knew, or at least the only ones she really wanted to use. After we got the vacuum we went to the wrong mansion at the wrong

time. Carla said I should go in first, and that the key to
the mansion was under a flowerpot by the door. I found
the key and went in. But inside, a woman wearing a
white robe was vacuuming. She screamed when she saw
me. I said I was a cleaning lady, though I knew it was a
dumb thing to say because she was already cleaning,
which meant we were in the wrong mansion. She yelled
at me to get out, that I was supposed to be there on
Tuesday. I said I was sorry and I got out. I ran back to
the truck where Carla and Liz were waiting and I told
them what had happened and they just laughed at me.
Liz called the woman in the robe a bad name without
even knowing what she looked like. In the next house
we went to I had to scrub dog pee off a carpet while a
cocker spaniel watched me from the cage where his
owners kept him locked up all day. I cleaned up the pee
on the carpet, and then I saw the puddle of pee the dog
was standing in. I let him out of there to clean out the
cage and at that point I realized I might as well let the
dog out of the house altogether, which I did, and which
I felt good about, but which I also figured ended my
career as a cleaning lady, so I found the master bathroom, filled the bath with a couple inches of hot water,
and warmed up my feet. There were six bottles of sham-
poo on the edge of the bathtub, each of which had
something called jojoba in it. Back in the truck, I told

Carla and Liz that I quit. Carla gave me five bucks and I was fine with it because of what I'd been able to do for the dog, which nobody ever said anything about afterward, so I assume he hit the woods for good where he became wild again and sired lots of mutts. I thought Liz would be mad or say something mean to me when I told her I quit but she didn't. She just ate a sandwich and said nothing. I noticed that Liz had some teeth missing, and that her missing teeth forced her to chew only with the right side of her mouth, which made me forget about how mean she'd been earlier. You have to be tough to be a cleaning lady, tough in a way I guess I wasn't.

COYOTES IN THE PARK

Coyotes live in the wilderness but they also live in big-city parks. The sound of a pack of coyotes can be ominous (see OMINOUS) or it can be thrilling. Animals perk up when they hear coyotes. Some animals get scared by the sound of coyotes, while others rush off to join the pack. Let's say you're sitting on the porch of your uncle's mansion and it's sunset and the coyotes start making noise somewhere in the distance. You hear yelps and high-pitched howls in one direction, and they'll start up all at once and then drop right back off. Right after that you hear another group of coyotes calling to the first coyote pack, responding, talking coyote, from someplace else. The sound of coyotes might cause you to feel strangely lonely, especially if you're prone to getting lonely right before you go to bed (see LONELY). Let's say your uncle starts howling back at the coyotes. He will howl, he will bark, and he will decide to visit the casino. But let's say you've once again snuck into the abandoned Victorian in the park downtown with your friend Ned, and by the light of a flashlight the two of you are looking through an old book you found in the top-floor bedroom when the coyotes start howling. If it's just you and Ned and you're already a little nervous since you're in a place where you're not supposed to be and the coyotes sound like they're close—they sound like they must be living in one of the old trees you know of in the park that's right outside the Victorian—you'll feel afraid. If the book you're reading is a huge old dictionary and the page you're flipped to is the page with the definition of COYOTE (see COINCIDENCE), and you hear four legs coming up the creaking wooden stairs, the tack-tack-tack of a dog's toenails outside the room you're in, and the door to the room is open, the flashlight beam will shake in your hand and your body will be frozen in fear. You may become sure you're about to die. Ned may have a breakdown (see DOWN, BREAKING). If it's a coyote coming up the stairs, you will have to fight it off. If it's the guard dog coming up the stairs with his tail between his legs, calm Ned down and leave before the guard dog works up his courage and decides he's bad.

CRISPY OLD PLASTIC

Forts designed and made from scratch are a lot better than the store-bought forts made of plastic parts that you take out of a box and put together according to a diagram. For some reason, plastic forts are replacing the old-fashioned hammer-and-nails variety, especially in neighborhoods like the one my uncle lived in. One good thing about a plastic fort is that it will never rot. Over many years, though, the plastic walls will slowly be crisped by sunlight. If you walk the woods and weed-buried fields along the outskirts of suburban neighborhoods, it's only a matter of time before you'll find an old plastic fort overturned and half-hidden by weeds. Finding one of these abandoned structures, you will feel the need to learn about who lived in it. At one time, you'll think, this fort was ruled by two children, and those children imagined it was a castle. You'll stand there looking into the dirt-filled corners, in light coming through the plastic, and you'll try to imagine what she looks like now, the grown-up girl who played in this fort, who carved flowers in its walls and the next day abandoned it.

CONSTRUCTION SITE

A construction site is a place where workers and machines are building a new building or tearing one down, or both. If you play a lot of hide-and-seek, odds are you've played it at a construction site or you've at least considered it as a possibility, but the first thing the construction workers do when they start a new construction site is put up a huge fence around it so that kids can't come in there and play with their tools or steal supplies for their treehouses. Construction-site hide-and-seek is best played at night just as long as there's no night watchman or any other kind of Daddy (see DADDIES) around to bust you. Besides that there's only one other thing you need to be careful about: don't get swallowed up by a pipe. I remember I was once running full-tilt across a construction site at night. Ned was chasing me. I vaulted a pile of two-by-fours, swung on a chain that was dangling from a metal beam, crawled through a concrete tunnel partially filled with mud, got up, ran some more, then saw a wide plastic hole in the ground and stopped to take a look. Ned was way behind me by then so I had a little time. Well, the plastic hole, it turned out, was a pipe in the ground that went down really far. I realized it was a great place to hide, so I lowered myself into it and dangled from the rim of the pipe. I was able to dangle there for a minute or two before my arms started to give out and I pulled myself out of it. Then I called Ned over and showed him the pipe. We dropped a rock down there and never heard it hit, so we established that the hole was very deep. Around a month later Ned came up to me and said that some kid in the first grade had fallen in there and gone down at least three hundred feet and died. When I think about that kid I feel sick.

CANOEING PONDS

Let's get one thing out of the way first: snakes love taking shelter beneath overturned canoes. Most people store their canoes on the edges of ponds, bottom up, paddles below, everything ready for a quick launch. So many people have done this for so long that snakes have gotten used to it and have taught each other about the shaded grass under the canoe. Whenever you turn over a canoe, you should be prepared to encounter a snake. The snake, when its canoe has been overturned, will make a quick break for the water. Do not stand between the snake and the water. Allow the snake to go, and always check for any more snakes that may have been trapped in the canoe as you flipped it over. The last thing you want is to realize you're sharing the canoe with a snake while you're out there in the middle of the pond. Once you've conducted the snake check, you're all ready to canoe. If it's a windy day on the pond, be ready to encounter the reeds and the cattails. If it's a calm, placid day on the pond and the water looks like a piece of glass, you're in for an easy paddle. You get around in the canoe by paddling or by pushing off the bottom with a long stick. But be careful: if you're using a stick to pole around the pond, say you're trying to be silent so that you can bag a bullfrog or two, take care not to push yourself into deep water where your pole cannot touch the bottom. In this case, when you try to push off the bottom with your pole, you will fall overboard.

CANOEISTS IN THE REEDS, RESCUING

If you listen closely to the reeds and cattails around the banks of a pond on a breezy day in spring, you might just hear the beautiful sound of grass blades singing. The hum of many reed and cattail stalks singing in the breeze is like music. The hum rises and falls and stops on notes, just like a bugle. At first, you might think you're hearing a flautist in the reeds and you may want to find her. If you hear someone whimpering somewhere off in the humming reeds, get ready for a rescue operation. Beginner canoeists, not having checked their boats for snakes, go out on windy days and get blown sideways into the reeds and the cattails that grow along the edge of the pond. If you hear a canoeist whimpering, it's because she's hung up in the reeds where it's dark and where strange things like to live. In the reeds and cattails you find green, spherical seedpods covered in tiny hairs that explode when you touch them, thick webs with fat black-and-yellow spiders at their centers, and complicated nests like tiny treehouses that are guarded by tiny birds. There are tangles of water snakes, beehives, and the FLYNN GUIDE's least favorite: the cocklebur. A beginner canoeist blown sideways into the reeds and cattails will flail and paddle in a panic and get more and more stuck. She won't know that the key to getting free of the reeds is to stay calm, wait for the wind to take a breath between blows, and pole backwards the same way she came in. If you hear a canoeist whimpering in the reeds, yell out that you're coming and head in the direction of the whimpering. Carefully stand up in your boat, slowly so you don't tip it, and scan the reeds. This is how you find the lost canoeist. You'll scare off all the bullfrogs you might have been trying to catch, but it's important to remember that you, too, were once blown helplessly into the reeds and would have died if it hadn't been for your uncle coming to the rescue. It's good to have a chance to repay your debt to the canoeing community. Once you find her, get the lost canoeist in to your canoe. She may not want to paddle after what she's been through. Tie the lost canoeist's boat to yours and paddle out of the reeds. It's a good idea to ask the canoeist questions to calm her down and distract her from her recent ordeal, questions like, "Do you often come out to the pond?" "Do you know where to find arrowheads?" "Did you once have a plastic fort where you carved flowers on the inside?"

CREATIVE ACQUISITION OF EASY SNACKS

When you've got a lot of things on your to-do list and you hope to do them all in one day, you better hope you're prepared with some kind of an easy snack you can reach for in order to keep your blood sugar up. If your day involves working in the deep woods of a mid-city park, in a stand of trees from whose canopies you can see skyscrapers, you might consider routing your approach to the park in such a way that you pass by a couple of street vendors selling hot food. You should especially be routing yourself past those street vendors on days that are windy. Street vendors are a distractible bunch of people as a whole. When the wind blows steadily, say on a warm spring day before a thunderstorm, street vendors are often so distracted by the dispersal of napkins and plastic utensils that you can just walk up and pluck a swollen hot dog right off the hot grill with your fingers, then disappear unnoticed. That's an easy snack. Other easy snacks include granola bars and small bags of nuts. At Ned's house, snacks were always easy. His mom made popcorn that had yellow cheese mixed in with the popped kernels and she'd bring a bowl of it to us every time we were over there. She even bought us pizza once, then ate with us while we watched a movie in the living room.

CAMPFIRE

A fire built outside. This is very important: you build a campfire outside, never in. It may be cold in the treehouse, and you may build a fire in there to stay warm, but believe me, you will regret it. Here's how a campfire works: heat comes from burning wood, cardboard boxes, leaves, or tires. Plastic is no good. Your warmth comes from the heat of whatever you're burning. Old wood is what's best to burn. Old wood comes from the pile that sits beneath your treehouse, where it stays mostly dry. Start with little sticks and work your way up. Use gasoline if you want, but take your hat off if you're going to start your fire with gas, and, if you're a girl, tie your hair up in a ponytail. I once wrote an entire glossary just about campfires, but in the amount of time it took you to read the glossary you could have built a campfire and learned about campfires that way, and when I realized that, I burned what I wrote about campfires in a campfire. If I had it to do over I don't think I'd have burned what I wrote since it's wrong to burn books and since you never know when you might want to read about a campfire instead of actually building one.

COINCIDENCE

When you see a connection between two separate events. Coincidence is a link made up by your mind. Any two things can be a coincidence if they occur near one another in time and if a person believes these two things have one specific thing in common and everything else not in common. Some people, when they see a coincidence, point to God—as if something or someone planned for two unrelated things to happen, for someone to see those two things happen, and for that person to draw a link between the two things and find meaning there.

CAST

A word with several meanings. If you're near water you might cast a pole, cast a net, or cast a line, and the purpose of casting all these things is to bring something back to you. A different kind of cast is the cast of a play. Then there's the cast of your memories, a cast which might also help you bring the forgotten stories back. The cast of this glossary so far: my uncle, El Hondero, Ned, the Midway Raptors, Carla and Liz, a dog breeder, some dogs, a clown, street vendors, a vaporized child and a vaporized horse, a dead boy in a pipe, some normal children and some normal horses, several snakes, strangers in the outfield, my parents living in a school bus, and a canoeist lost in the reeds. A cast is also what I wore on my arm for six weeks after a rotten board caused me to fall out of my treehouse.

CYCLE

Spring, summer, autumn, winter, spring, summer, autumn. Storm, heat, storm, cold, heat, storm, night, lightning. The first list is a cycle, the second list is more like chaos because you can never really know what will come next. What's interesting is that chaos is embedded within cycles. Storms, for instance, happen regularly in spring. And this: grow hair, shed hair, grow hair, shed hair. This was the cycle of my uncle's cat. If you didn't know anything about cycles, you might be sitting in your chair petting your cat and looking out your window one day in October and you would say, "What a coincidence! That tree starts losing its leaves just as this cat starts to shed its hair!" and you would waste time wondering, for a while, what this coincidence could mean for you.

COOKOUT

One of the first signs of spring, a cookout is when people start fires in grills and then the cookout attendees stand around the grill smelling the meat, commenting on the smell, and drinking alcoholic beverages. Sometimes a cookout also involves organized games such as lawn darts and croquet. Sometimes the attendees light fireworks after the sun has gone down, the meat has been cooked, and the children have begun playing flashlight tag. One time I was at a cookout at Ned's house. It was late, and we were playing flashlight tag with a couple of his neighbors. After a while, their parents came and picked them up and then it was just me and Ned and Ned's parents sitting in the dark backyard. Ned's parents asked me how I'd come to know so much about nocturnal animals, and that's when I realized I'd been talking for a long time about the bat colony I'd seen in the woods while nobody else was saying anything. Ned just sat there smiling because he liked hearing about weird things but also because I was the fastest runner in tag and I'd been on his team. Then my uncle showed up with a huge firework in a bag. He was late because he'd been looking for this special kind of rocket. Ned's parents said it was okay for Ned to light it, so he lit it, but first he went into the shed and got every-body a baseball helmet to wear during the explosion. The boom echoed, and there were lots of little lights. Ned's mom screamed. A door slammed from the next house over and a fat man with no shirt on came out and started yelling at us through the fence.

COOLER SNAKE
A snake found in an abandoned cooler.

CREPUSCULAR
The word CREPUSCULAR describes animals that are neither nocturnal nor usually found in the day.

Crepuscular animals come out right at dawn and dusk, when the sun is gone over the horizon but somehow light still lingers like a ghost of the sun, or when the moon has long risen, raced across the sky and set, when you can still see stars but the sky is going from black to ultramarine. Crepuscular animals appear in this short-lived light and disappear when the light is more decisive.

CHICKEN HAWK

This is a raptor that favors the common barnyard chicken as prey. Somehow the fox escaped being called the chicken dog. No one can explain why. Language is a mystery. Also CHICKEN HAWK can refer to an adult male who is attracted to young boys. This slang term originated in Little League bleachers as a reference term, used by parents, referring to strange adult men spectating from beyond the outfield.

COURT ORDER

Have you ever wondered why there are some things you can do and others you can't? Most good people have a natural idea of what's right and what's wrong, and so they can figure out how to live the type of life that doesn't hurt others. Most children, as a rule, have not figured out what's right and what's wrong quite as well as most adults, but some children have a pretty good idea of right and wrong from the beginning and only have to learn the subtler rules, the ones made by adults in courts. Who decided, for example, that it's wrong for a child to build a treehouse in a public park? The court did. The thing is, there are lots of things you can do that the court hasn't made a decision about, and so often you just can't know. You don't think you need to know, either, because you have your own idea, but then the authorities come and see you doing something they don't have a name for but still they think that thing is wrong, and then they go to court and make a rule about it or figure out a way to make it part of a rule that already exists. For this reason there are courts all over the place, and each city has several of its own. Every court I've seen is inside of a stone building with stone columns in front. At dusk, little birds fly into the courthouse chimney. Stone steps lead up to the court entrance, which is usually guarded by two stone lions and a policeman. Once you get past the lions and the policeman and you're inside the stone building, walk until you find the two big wooden doors with frosted glass windows in them. Behind these big wooden doors is the courtroom—the wooden room where the judge in the black robe hits the wooden block with his wooden mallet. People go to the courtroom to listen to the judge talk before he hits the wood with his mallet. When he says your name, you stand up and he says his thing and smacks his mallet and you're supposed to react. If the judge orders you to clean up garbage for a week because for the second time in a month you were caught building a treehouse in a public park, it's better to thank the judge and leave than to explain to him that you were actually building a blind from which you could watch birds—it was my uncle's idea that we say it was a blind, and he'd dressed up in a suit and come down to the court with me to explain it to the judge, but also to say that if my mother were still on this earth she'd have been the first to teach me some respect for private property—either way you'll be issued court-ordered community service. The judge can order anyone to do anything he wants. He has an old woman named Patty who he sends to carry out court orders. You should hope that he does not unleash Patty, or anyone like her, to come get you. If you see her, don't even try to run. She is much more powerful than she looks. The best plan is to do as she says, act nice, and nod at the strange things she says to you. Patty is about five and a half feet tall and has short gray hair that looks like it's glued to her scalp. She wears between ten and twenty jingling bracelets you can hear from fifteen feet away, carries a black leather bag over her shoulder, and holds a thick stack of papers against her chest as she walks—though she doesn't walk like anyone else. She waddles, never changing her pace, never actually bending her knees properly, and she always smells like soap. The scariest thing about Patty is her fingernails. Her fingernails are more a residue than a body part. She chews them past the cuticle, or else some disease is eating them away, but whatever the reason they're horrible and she likes to touch you with them. Her job, as she sees it, is to find you (she once found me in the dumpster behind the dollar store collecting cardboard for use as insulation) and to "find out how you're doin." If you run from her, she'll just find you again later, and when she does she'll have brought along the policeman who guards the court. When she finds you, she'll make you get in her red car, which is always parked around the corner. She'll make you get in there and she'll put on classical music and hum along to it while she fills out papers with a golden pen with a blunt end she chewed the gold off of. You'll spend an hour in the car answering questions about your uncle, questions about what you eat, questions about any bruises or cuts you have on your body (which she'll touch with those nails). You should answer as sincerely as possible while always making it sound like your life with your uncle is as good as you can imagine life could get. Patty will smile and act like she cares about you and her whole act will be as fake as her teeth but you have to act like you believe her or else you'll end up at an orphanage in Oklahoma. Don't be tricked into thinking that she knows about you or that she will tell you anything useful about your absent parents. You are in the

custody of your uncle, is all she will say, as if you didn't
understand that fact very clearly. She will touch you with
those hands and look at you like you're the dog with wheels
instead of back legs and she'll say how "confused" you must
be and how "sad" it is that your mother "was who she was"
but Patty won't ever say anything that makes any sense.

DRAFT

This is another word with many meanings. (1) My uncle's
boat, which was a canoe, had a shallow draft. This meant
that there was very little of the boat that spent the whole
time beneath the surface of his pond. A shallow draft
allows easy turning but offers almost no resistance to the
pressures of the wind. The gentlest of breezes will push
the boat sideways across the pond and into a thicket of
snake-filled cattails. (2) In Little League, when the
coaches pick teams by looking at a list of names and circling the ones they want on their team, they refer to what
they're doing as "drafting talent." (3) A special kind of
draft known as an updraft is a gust of air blowing directly upward, often at the forefront of big storms, and
always in the middle of them. Picture a column of air.
Updrafts make rain go up as opposed to down, and then
the rain freezes and comes down as hail, like it did one
day in spring when I was canoeing on my uncle's pond in
the hopes of spotting the snapping turtle. Although the

untrained eye sees all pieces of hail as identical, close inspection reveals that there are four standard shapes of hail, each with dual subvarieties. There exists a gypsy psychic who collects hail, studies the shape of each piece, and uses this information to talk in detail about specific events that have not yet happened.

DREAMS OF THE BETTA FISH

If you use the fish-tasting method of nightmare aversion, you must prepare yourself to deal with the following inevitable side effect of using the Betta Fish: the Betta Fish Dream. In Betta Fish dreams, you will be in an enormous tank of bottomless water with an enormous Betta Fish. You will be much smaller than the Betta Fish. The Betta Fish will be like a submarine compared to you, and it will be terrifying. In your Betta Fish dreams, you will sometimes find the courage to coexist with the Betta Fish. You will find that you have no fear, at all, of the fish's flowing fins or its compassionless gaze. You will float there in awe of its beauty. Sometimes you will paddle your hands, and your strokes will take you shooting like an arrow through the water. Sometimes you will expand to the size of the Betta Fish, other times you will watch the fish change into other things or shrink to the size that it is, in reality, floating in its little tank across the room from your bed. Still other times you will find yourself asleep, staring at the Betta Fish in the bottomless bowl of water, and you will fear it. When you at last awake and look over at the Betta Fish floating innocently in its bowl of water, you will be able to tell— in its eyes—that it knows you have just now dreamt of it. It's not just me who has had the Betta Fish Dream. My cousin Isabella used to have it, too.

DADDIES

A Daddy is a false authority. There are many different kinds of authorities someone may talk about, like, "The authority on grilling steaks is Bob," or, "I'm not the authority on huts made of mammoth bone, though I'd bet money they held up better than tepees," and if your uncle says, simply, "The authorities are on their way," he is referring to the police who show up when high-powered fireworks are detonated within city limits, when a mansion has burned down, when strangely behaving people wander into the outfield at Little League games, or when an adult at a cookout notices that his or her child has disappeared while playing flashlight tag. A Daddy, on the other hand, is a guy who thinks he's an authority figure but is not. Let's say you're in your treehouse playing dice with Ned when a man appears from the bushes at the base of the tree and says you're not allowed to be up there. Let's say you then ask him who he is and why he thinks you can't be up there. If he says he's a fireman but doesn't look like one and if when you tell him you're not coming down he starts to come up the ladder, you've got a Daddy on your hands.

DERELICT CHILD

A derelict child, also known as a wild child, is a child who has been living in the outdoors, away from civilization, and has learned how to exist as one of the animals. Wild children have long hair and skin caked with dirt, are commonly naked and like to eat raw meat. Some wild children have been raised by wolves, others by coyotes. Some wild children have been stolen by animals at birth. Wild children have their own idea of what's right and what's wrong. Several wild children, for example, have been captured in the act of freeing farm animals. Some wild children don't speak any human language. Others speak the language they spoke as babies. Some children become wild children after getting hopelessly lost and then staying lost while surviving off their animal instincts. El Hondero once told me that he spent a whole winter as a wild child. He disappeared from a hog roast when he was nine and came back when he was eleven, said he'd gone for a really long hike. My uncle saw a wild child once. He was sitting on the porch of his mansion practicing the bugle when he saw, by the edge of a pond far off by the tree line, a naked boy burst from the forest, catch a goose with his hands, and return to the woods with it. He summoned the authorities, who searched the forest around the pond and found little footprints in the mud but never found the child.

DOWN, BREAKING
Someone's driving his car someplace and the engine stops working and he has to pull over and call a tow truck. That's a breakdown. During the draft, Ned got picked to be on a team called The Crushers because their coach had picked him randomly and it turned out that The Crushers were a team for which a gang of five bullies played, bullies who knew Ned and had beaten him up on numerous occasions, so when Ned heard that he'd been drafted to that team he had a breakdown. Mostly the breakdown looked like crying and yelling, though it also looked like him taking his dad's shovel out to the backyard and digging himself a grave beneath an apple tree.

DIGGING IN WOOD: WHITTLING
To whittle is to sculpt wood into things like spears and knives and shafts for arrows. Some people whittle just for fun, as Ned discovered while digging his grave, for he found beneath the tree a tiny wooden horse that someone had whittled and then buried. The finding of the wooden horse took his mind off his impending doom and led to a

thorough archaeological excavation of the dirt around the apple tree, the disturbance of the roots, the falling of the unripe apples, and the breakdown of Ned's mother. My uncle brought home two whittled chairs one summer. They showed up, stayed on the lawn for a month, and then he pawned them because the bets really weren't going his way. The two chairs were whittled from cherry by a nearby authority on wood. I remember there was a week or so where I forgot all about the treehouse and just sat in a wooden chair beside my uncle, who was sitting in another. I think he was lonely that summer, because his daughter Isabella had sent a letter saying she'd met an astronaut in France and might move with him to Florida. I remember feeling the cuts in the wood with my fingers and trying to picture what tool it was that had made them. Get a well-whittled chair, put it out on the lawn when it turns to summer, and you won't want to move from it. At least that's how it was for me and my uncle.

E____? WORD UNKNOWN

There's a word for the study of how natural landscapes came to be shaped the way they are. There's a way for specialists to look out across a meadow and read the humps and divots that make up the surface of the earth, then go on to describe a sequence of natural events that caused the earth to look the way it does. Why are there more trees over here than over there? Why so much of a slope on this side of the meadow and no slope at all on the other side? Turns out there are people who can tell you. They're experts in ancient forces of nature: prehistoric tornadoes, ancient rains, archaic gales . . . but I can't remember what they're called. I think their name starts with E.

EXPLORATION OF BLACKNESS

People use the word BLACK to describe many things that are not actually black: blackberries and black people and blacktop are three good examples, but the best example is probably the night. The color black does not reflect light, so a black object actually has the sun's light kept in it (see BRIGHTNESS OF SUNLIGHT). Photo paper burned with light turns black, a tire is black for a while but then it fades to gray, black is lightning-struck wood and burned buildings. The black of burned wood never fades but starts to shine over time. Black is always the color of your pupil, and black is the color the sun becomes after you've looked straight at it for two seconds. The true nature of black will always be up for debate. Sit outside in lawn chairs at dusk or at dawn and watch the transition from day to night, the transition mistakenly referred to as light to dark. Watch the colors that appear during this time of transition. Think of how those colors feel through the sharp eyes of crepuscular animals or through the big, yellow eyes of nocturnal ones, then hear how it sounds to say that something is as black as the night.

EARLIER HILLBILLIES

The people who lived in the double-wide trailer a half mile southwest of my uncle's mansion were hillbillies. This meant they gathered near foul-smelling fires, drank in the daytime, had fights, and played music long into the night. Hillbillies have agreed not to think too much about questions like IS BLACK ACTUALLY BLACK or IS WHITE ACTUALLY WHITE, perhaps because they see things around them as complicated enough as is, or maybe because they think there comes a time in your life when you know all you need to know, or maybe the hillbillies just long for an earlier time: a time with fewer authorities, when things were simpler for hillbillies, when everyone burned their trash and children fell freely from dangerous treehouses built in old trees that are gone now and replaced by mansions.

ENLARGER

A five-foot-tall piece of equipment that prints photographs. The photographer uses his enlarger in a pitch-dark closet or in a closet with only a tiny red light because white light messes up his process. He takes his roll of film, which has tiny photographs called NEGATIVES burned into it, and slides it into the mouth of the projector (the slot beneath the enlarger's lightbulb eye). Then he turns off all the lights (except the red one), takes a sheet of photographic paper from the dark plastic envelope that keeps the paper in darkness, puts the paper beneath the negative and the eye, and turns on the enlarger. The light shines through the negative and gives the special paper an invisible burn in the shape of a picture. Then he turns the enlarger off and puts the special paper in a chemical bath and swishes it around for a while until the photograph emerges from the special paper. It took me a while to figure out how the enlarging process worked, especially since I couldn't ask my uncle about it, and everything I know comes from a teenager named Brad who works at the photo shop. When Brad asked why I was so curious, it all just came out. You really never know who you will tell things to and who you won't. My uncle had only ever told me my dad had disappeared and wouldn't be coming back, I was my uncle's responsibility and would be until I was eighteen, which was five years away. I had become my uncle's responsibility when my dad disappeared. That was all I ever got, and I knew not to ask any more. I knew that it had something to do with the fight between my uncle and my dad, the one I saw years ago, in the kitchen, and I knew the fight had something to do with my mom. Some time after I moved in with my uncle I stopped thinking about my dad. I don't know when and I don't know why, but I began to think of my father as dead, except being dead, in the case of my mother, meant people thought about you more often than if you'd just disappeared. I know my uncle thought about my mother because he kept a picture of her on the mantel and I saw him look at it a few times. He didn't keep any pictures of my father on the mantel. After a while it was as if my father had never existed, as if I was the son of my uncle. Then came the day that I found the photo enlarger in the basement along with the old photographs and I needed to make sense of what I saw in the pictures. You need to have been alive to be in a photograph, and so I told Brad that the enlarger was proof that my father had existed and might continue to exist. The discovery of the photographs made my father more than a blurry memory of a man by the banks of a pond.

EXPECTATION

The brain spends a huge amount of time expecting things. The brain lives on patterns the way a blade of grass lives on sunlight. When you look at a single leaf on a twig and you know right off the bat you're seeing a tree, that's you EXPECTING without KNOWING. Other, more complicated expectations are the more interesting ones because of how often they backfire. For example, one day I was in my tree fort when Ned came up through the trapdoor with a bag of lemons in his backpack. I said something like "Hooray lemonade" and Ned then pointed through the window at a group of kids who played for the Crushers and who were coming at us through the bushes. We had expected to juice those lemons, but it turned out we needed to use them against the Crushers: put a nail through a lemon, whip it out the window of a treehouse, bean a kid with it—that kid will probably move on. My uncle learned to stop expecting things from Isabella because she kept changing her mind all the time. One day she was moving to Florida, the next she was back at my Uncle's house with the astronaut in tow, the next she had an apartment in the city, the next she was gone, nowhere to be found, then the next she was back again, and so on. When he expected her and the astronaut to move into the mansion with us, he started building an addition. That was a mistake. People don't often say what they're really going to do. Ned told me he was going to help me get revenge on the Crushers, but then a little while later I saw him walking down the street with them like they were his friends. When I told Isabella I'd help get her canoe out of the reeds, though, I helped her. I was six years younger than Isabella, and my boat had less draft, but she knew I could paddle hard and she knew that I liked her so when she saw me coming she expected she'd be saved.

FACTS

A FACT is a statement of truth as opposed to a statement that is questionable. Facts make up what we call KNOW-LEDGE. On the other hand, lots of people go around living their life with certain facts drilled into their brains, facts that cause them to behave certain ways, facts they've either never questioned or have given up questioning. I'll list a few items that might, at face value, given what you know up to this point, appear factual.

1. Horses head for the woods during storms.
2. Plastic forts are quickly abandoned.
3. Balloons are often lost in the wind.
4. My uncle played the bugle.
5. Spring comes before summer.
6. Animals love the dark.
7. In the dark, you print photos using light.
8. Gravity exists, but not for balloons, and not if you've been turned to smoke.
9. Lemons with nails through them hurt when they hit you.
10. A wild child can catch a goose by hand.

Of those ten things, only two are facts. Statement 1, for instance, is not a fact, because it's not a fact everywhere. That's another thing about facts—if it's an actual fact, it will be true everywhere. I've heard about horses in Mongolia that seek the shelter of a cave before the shelter of a tree when they feel a storm coming. I've heard about a boy in Georgia who slept every night in his plastic fort until one day he grew too large to get back in. Statement 3 is, in fact, a fact. It is a fact that here, and in a different state, and in a different country, balloons are lost by their handlers. The first, sad fact we learn in this life is that balloons fly away. That fact and the fact of gravity are probably the first two facts we're forced to confront at a very early age. "You must go inside now. No more playing outside," may sound like a fact, but it isn't. If instead someone says: "Unless you go inside right now, you'll be totally vaporized by lightning. Look there—there's lightning in that cloud," you will look at the cloud, consider the source (Is he an alarmist or does he often have courage? Fact: not all astronauts are courageous), and decide whether or not to risk it.

FAULTY WISHING

You must wish correctly if you want your wish to come true. Let's say you're sitting with your uncle on the porch and you're watching a storm come in. The horses are moving to the cover of the stand of cedars, and a little bunch of blue balloons has come loose from a birthday party somewhere and is flying skyward and sideways. Let's say your uncle tells you that wishes come true if you wish upon balloons you spot floating off to the balloon afterlife. Let's say he tells you that he's already wished on two of those four balloons and that you should wish on the other two, quick, and you wish. You say, "I wish I could find out why my dad left," and your uncle sighs. He sighs and shakes his head and says that your wish was a dumb one, not just because the wish was dangerous but because—and by reading this you're learning the easy way—that by saying a wish aloud you are cursing it. This is especially the case with wishing on balloons. After he has corrected you, he might say, "Wish for something sensible if you're going to wish. Wish for money," and you don't want to, but you want to keep the peace with him, and so you pretend to wish for money. He looks at you and believes you are wishing for money. Your fake wish is that your uncle wins at the horse races so that he can pay off the expensive addition to the mansion, but your real wish, the deeper wish, is that everything in your life would change for good. You wish for anything else because your attempts to change your world have so far come to nothing. You place your wish on the fourth balloon just before it disappears behind a distant row of trees and then, in the next instant, at the exact moment when the fourth blue balloon disappears, a bolt of lightning strikes a dead tree by the pond and sets it aflame. From a hole in the flaming tree pop four little balls of fire which go arcing into the pond, landing with sizzles in the water, and then, an instant later, four fish jump from the water in quick succession. You learn, then and there, that flaming birds change to fish when you put them out in a pond, and so you could say that fish live not just in ponds but also in trees.

FREE FALL

When she jumps out of a helicopter, airplane, or hot-air balloon, she starts free-falling toward the earth at a tremendous speed. She plunges through clouds. She gets a good look at the fields and the forests, the immense blues and greens and browns, the whites of the clouds below her, and then at some point she deploys her parachute. My uncle and I were waiting there when Isabella landed in the field at the little airport. You couldn't help but look at her and feel happy. The astronaut landed right after Isabella, but he wasn't smiling. To him, the free fall was nothing special. After the free fall was the first time Isabella had really looked at me since the day she'd met the astronaut. Her parachute was made from the same stuff as El Hondero's weather balloons: light, multicolored material that catches the eye from miles away, reflecting sunlight. Parachutes can serve other, secondary functions, such as housing for gypsies. Of all the showy and mysterious sorts of structures human beings live in, the gypsy-style parachute house (see GYPSY PARACHUTE HOUSE) is by far the most wonderful.

FANDALAHALANAI

This is a string of syllables you use to stop authorities (or Daddies) who are trying to interfere with your plans. When I was little, before Ned joined the Crushers, me and Ned and Isabella had to use the magic syllables a lot. Me and Isabella had other words, too, and we wrote them down, but now I can't remember them. Isabella made up a whole fairy tale to explain my existence and why we could do magic. Isabella said that she'd been out in the woods picking berries when she was in third grade and that she'd found me sleeping in a basket. She said she brought me home and hid me in the basement, and that I had special psychic powers which was why people thought I was a weirdo. The story would change a little every time she told it but I'd always go along with it no matter who it was she was telling it to. She once said we could communicate telepathically, and that we dreamed the same dreams, that we'd both had the same Betta Fish nightmare. Then, one day, she stopped telling the fairy tale and started telling the real one, about how my mom had died and my dad had disappeared. FANDALAHALANAI, back when it was a word that had power, was something you could call someone to his face and he wouldn't know what you were doing to him as long as you said it in a casual way. If you said it while wiggling your left pinky-toe and you clapped twice after saying it, the FANDALAHALANAI was given extra power. If three people did it at once, you were sure to get what you wanted. One time we were in the basement with a bunch of old film we'd found in the closet, the same place where I'd found the enlarger, my uncle's old skis, and two five-gallon tanks of gasoline. We had the film taped up on a window so we could go through the negatives one by one and try to figure out the story of where my father had taken these pictures when we heard my uncle coming down the stairs. We all did FANDALAHALANAI at once and it worked. He turned around and went back up.

FALLACY

A fallacy is something you believe to be true but which is not actually a fact, and believing which brings disaster. To actually believe Fandalahalanai works—instead of just saying you believe it and really knowing that it only worked because of coincidence—would be a fallacy. The ultimate fallacy is the one held by the person who thinks he can fly. In the case of the astronaut floating in space, it is not a fallacy that he can fly, but for everyone else, even pilots, to adopt as a fact the idea that you can fly is to invite calamity. It is a fallacy that you love someone if you say you love him but then you run away.

FLIGHT
The act of moving through the air without touching the ground and without using anything like vines or monkey bars. Also, the act of running away from something or someone quickly, and by any means necessary.

GYPSIES
Gypsies travel by means of Winnebagos or similar motor caravans, and they travel in groups. The largest, or "King," Winnebago will be followed by a collection of beat-up vehicles covered in countless dents both large and small, vehicles belching black smoke, vehicles that appear as if they've recently broken down. Gypsies are sort of like hillbillies but much more superstitious and also much more ready to accept alternative ways of thinking. Gypsies excel at finding ways to hustle (see METHODS OF THE HUSTLE). This makes people who aren't gypsies jealous (see ANGER, JEALOUS),

including most of the people living in the mansions near my uncle's. Often, I'd be on my way back from my treehouse when I'd see a police car stopped at the Winnebago village, the policemen hassling some gypsies about camping there. Getting hassled is nothing new for gypsies, though. They're used to it. Gypsies get hassled everywhere they go and will just move on to somewhere else once they're done with their hustle.

GYPSY PARACHUTE HOUSE

If you happen to be lucky enough to find yourself in the vicinity of people living in a house made of an old parachute, do yourself a favor and ask them if you can go inside. When the sun is shining through the fabric, being inside of a parachute house feels like you're in the middle of a bowl of jelly beans. When it's storming outside, being in a parachute house is like being inside the body of a living thing. In my experience, the owners of parachute houses are gypsies, though there are almost certainly owners from all kinds of backgrounds. As for the gypsies, they always knew how to anchor the parachute securely in the ground using whittled-down wooden stakes and sewn-in grommets, so I was never scared, no matter how intense the storm. I remember one time being inside the parachute house right as a big storm was picking up. There were four gypsies playing music and singing. The parachute fabric was bouncing around us like an amoeba, and when it brushed up against our skin it got us wet. Then a piece of hail the size of a popcorn kernel punched a hole in the parachute and landed at my feet. One of the gypsies put down his flute, picked up the hailstone, and danced around with it pinched in his fingers, laughing as he danced. For gypsies, hail can be good luck, especially if it comes inside a parachute house.

GROATS

Cereal grains, kind of like oatmeal, that have been served to horses and which the horses have turned down. Some health-food stores package and sell the refused grains. Isabella ate a lot of groats one summer before she met the astronaut. She said she'd fallen in love with one of the guys who was living in a Winnebago a few miles down the road. She said the groats were healthy and good for her, but I knew she was just trying to look good for the guy in the Winnebago. One morning at breakfast, my uncle said that the guy in the Winnebago was a gypsy and Isabella said that actually he'd come from Seattle. I laughed because I thought it was funny that coming from Seattle meant you couldn't be a gypsy, but Isabella thought I was laughing at her so she got angry and threw a handful of groats.

GETTING IN CARS WITH STRANGERS

Of all the cautionary tales adults tell to children, the tale of the stranger's invitation is the all-time strongest. Usually he drives a white van in the story. He comes up alongside you as you're walking home alone and asks you if you need a ride. There are some variations. Sometimes the stranger is driving a beat-up station wagon and it's a woman instead of a man. Sometimes the stranger is dangling a piece of candy out the window of the car and the stupid child decides to go for the bait. Sometimes the van rolls up, the stranger asks the question, and against your better judgment you get in the van. Let's say you're walking home from your tree fort one day in spring. Let's say that you lost track of time on account of the fact that you were tricked into a wild goose chase by a passing child, and let's say, for the sake of the story, that the passing child's goose chase began as the fallacious claim that there would be a fistfight between two boys at the old dump on the far edge of the park, which ended with your going all the way there only to have the kid who led you there realize, at the last minute, that the fistfight was actually scheduled for tomorrow as opposed to today, and so you're walking home much later than you normally would, so late that the last mile of your walk, at the rate you're traveling, will be a walk in darkness. Let's say that you're looking at the sun and it's only a hand's breadth from the horizon, so you calculate it to be about an hour from dark, and you haven't even passed the laundromat yet, which puts you at least ninety minutes from home, and you start to freak out. If you'd planned ahead, you would have brought a knife, but as it is you might as well be walking naked through a chicken hawk's den. And let's say that's when the van rolls up alongside you—in that moment when you're most desperate—and let's say that the van is being driven by one of the hillbilly neighbors you've seen burning tires outside the trailer visible from your uncle's mansion. The hillbilly's wearing sunglasses, though it's crepuscular, and you glimpse, through a window in the side of the van, that there's a person back there, but all you can see is a shadow. You feel like you've seen the driver before, but you don't know where. The driver offers you a ride. What do you do? If you refuse the ride, you risk making this person an enemy, and you risk hurting his feelings. But still— there's a chance that it's a trick, that he won't drive that van back to your neighborhood and will end up taking you somewhere else, someplace terrible and unknown to you, someplace where there are people who want to chain you up and slowly cut off your arms and legs. But let's say you think about walking home by yourself, unarmed, in the dark, the predators watching you from the trees, and then you decide to chance the ride with the hillbillies—you open the van door and get in, and before you even have time to put on your seat belt the van is racing down the road doing fifty in a thirty. The van smells like a bathroom, and you look behind you and see not one but three people back there, in the darkness, holding large glass bottles. One of them is Carla the cleaning lady, and she's French-kissing the guy next to her. The driver grins at you, saying nothing, showing off the gold in his teeth, and turns up the heavy metal that's coming from the static on the radio. At this point you are regretting your decision, and you come to regret your decision even more when the van sails past your uncle's driveway. You would, at this point, ask to be let out of the van. You would politely tell the driver, who has just driven past your uncle's driveway, that you'd really like to be let out of the van please. You would want to cry. Then the driver says something unintelligible to the people in the back and they start laughing—you'd be saying your prayers then—if, however, the driver tells you not to worry, that he knows your uncle and that the two of them go way back, and that your uncle would want you to be along for the ride, and Carla passes you a bottle and you drink from it, you might begin to feel a little better. You drink the warm, flat beer and it's like a skunk peed in your mouth and the driver laughs at how you looked as you drank it and his laughter would make you mad, mad enough to where you chug the hot skunk-pee, you let it drip down your shirt, and the driver stops laughing. He turns up the heavy metal. You shut your eyes and try not to puke. The van turns off the main road and goes bouncing down a dirt track, falling into and out of foot-deep potholes. You're preparing yourself for death when, all of a sudden, the dirt road becomes a circular, dirt-filled field, a clearing surrounded by tall trees, and the driver of the van stomps the pedal to the floor. The stomping of the pedal to the floor forces you back into your seat and the passengers behind you to hoot like ghouls in a haunted house. The driver is cackling and you, you're screaming louder than you've ever screamed before, but the urge to flee has left you completely. You grip the seat beneath you as the driver wrenches the steering wheel to the left and the van goes sliding sideways toward the tree line at the far edge of the circular clearing. You are, at this point, peeing your pants, or maybe it's beer spilling from Carla's bottle. She's leaning up from the back and yelling something at the driver and you can't tell if it's happy or mad, and you wonder if you've become the victim of a collective suicide but then, at the last moment, the van gracefully curves its rear around so the front points toward the center of the mud pit as the whole van slides sideways around the center. Mud is slapping against the windows in brown, wet sheets as the van slides. The sun is almost down and the van slides seven, eight more times around the center. The donuts end too soon and you beg the driver for more. He says that enough is enough, and that it's time to go home. He takes off his sunglasses and you see that his is a kind but somehow sad, run-down sort of a face. He drives you home, where your uncle takes one look at the van and lets you inside without a question.

GOLD IN THE MOUTH

Gold doesn't flake, or crumble, or make a mark on paper. It just sits, coloring the light. Once it's out of the ground, people want their gold to be kept safe from thieves in a bank or in their mouth. Gold is also found in jewelry, coins, and the tip of my uncle's pen. Gold attracts gold. When the bandits came for Alberta Otter, they were looking for gold, and it was most likely dangling from their wrists as they knocked her door down. Gold makes a unique sound when tapped with other gold. I could hear, from my bedroom, when my uncle was working on a crossword puzzle in his chair in the living room. He'd tap the gold tip of his pen against his one golden molar when he was thinking hard about a word. Sunlight turns golden on the leaves of certain trees, at certain times of day, when all the dust floating around in your treehouse is visible. Once, when Isabella and the astronaut came to the mansion for lunch, we all went swimming off the dock. Isabella took off her golden engagement ring, put it on the wood of the dock, and jumped in the water. Then my uncle went in, and finally the astronaut. It was hot. The clouds looked like huge popcorn. Isabella's ring was sitting there on the dock, gleaming. I put the ring in my mouth and held it there for a long time, past when they all started looking for it. The astronaut was diving, kept coming up gasping, and Isabella saw me giggling with my mouth closed. That's how she guessed it.

GOOD MANNERS, THE IMPORTANCE OF

You could say that the first humans knew it was bad manners to poop in the middle of the trail, right where people had to walk. There's no doubt that good manners exist in the animal kingdom as well, and probably always have. A well-mannered dog, for example, won't eat from another dog's food bowl. If you find that you're about to do something that's bad manners, you'll feel a weird sickness in your stomach. If you feel like you're about to have bad manners, try a thought exercise and see if it doesn't help you shake off the urge. Here's an example of a thought exercise that might help you: It's Easter. Three kids are running across a lawn in pursuit of eggs and jelly beans, holding baskets full of what they've already found. They're running because they've realized that one of the places they forgot to check for loot is at the base of the old dead tree by the pond. The three children are running side by side. One of the kids trips on a root and falls, spilling her basket across a patch of mud and spitting from her mouth a few half-chewed beans when her body hits the ground.

The well-mannered kid will stop running, help the fallen girl to her feet, and give her half of his jelly beans. That tripping root could have appeared before the foot of any of the children, and it's not fair that she should be left with no jelly beans because it was she who tripped. The well-mannered thing to do is to share the jelly beans with the fallen girl. Bad manners would be to laugh and run ahead to the rotten tree, snatch the eggs hidden in its claw-like roots, and keep them all for yourself.

HAIL DAMAGE

One of the number-one gypsy hustles is traveling to areas that have been hailed on and repairing hail damage. In the spring, after it hails, expect to see gypsies. Expect to see them come in with signs advertising the dangers of hail damage: WHAT STARTS AS A NICK IN YOUR WIND-SHIELD CAN BECOME A SPIDERWEB CRACK AND SHATTER WITHOUT WARNING. LUCKY FOR YOU, EVEN THE MOST EXTENSIVE HAIL DAMAGE CAN BE REPAIRED IN JUST A FEW MINUTES BY A TECH-NICIAN WITH THE PROPER SPECIALIZED EQUIP-MENT. Or: DON'T SHOW UP TO A BUSINESS MEETING DRIVING A CAR THAT HAS BEEN PUM-MELED BY HAIL. YOU WILL APPEAR DESPERATE! DON'T DRIVE TO THE BODY SHOP AND BE OVER-CHARGED FOR A JOB BY SOMEONE WHO ISN'T A

SPECIALIST. He will repair your first dent for free, just because he's being nice, and has good manners. If you like how he fixed the first dent, though, it's bad manners not to have him do the rest of the dents. Find a gypsy near you, if he hasn't already found you, and ask him about hail-damage dent repair and glass filling. Nobody's better at repairing hail damage than a gypsy who has followed the severe weather with his family and tools in tow.

HAVE A BLOWOUT
A flat tire is a type of blowout. So is a huge party, like a cookout but with more people in attendance. A child of the word BLOWOUT is the term BLOWN-OUT, which is used to talk about a whole variety of things but ultimately is a way of describing your opinion about something. "Look at that. That place is totally blown-out. I can't believe they're raising children in there," said someone standing on the porch of his mansion as he pointed to a lonely double-wide trailer on a ridge, where four hillbillies could be seen throwing tires into a smoking campfire (see CAMPFIRE) and listening to country music on a boom box.

HEADSTONE
This can refer to a band some of my cousin Isabella's friends were in, to a rock thrown at somebody's head, or

to the big gray slab they put in the ground over where a body is buried. The band Headstone was a three-piece hardcore group that practiced in my uncle's basement one time. The music was loud and they were banging their heads as they played. When practice ended, one of the guitarists came upstairs and found me in the kitchen. He had a shaved, pimply head and wore a shirt that looked like it had come off a body in the morgue. I was looking at a map of the park that I'd made the day before, minding my own business, when he opened the fridge, stole one of my Cokes, and came over to the table. I remember his shirt, wet and warm with the pimple sweat, brushing up against my arm. Then I remember him saying, "I know you, young dude," and I remember him pointing at me while he spoke. "Your mom was batshit, dude, and then your pops bailed out." I remember wondering what he meant by telling me that my mom was made of bat shit. That was the last I saw or heard of the band Headstone. Headstones, however, you can still find anywhere. Headstones are a very specific kind of throwing rock in that they're selected with the intention of being thrown at somebody's head. You'll know the stone you have is a headstone if when you pick it up you become blind with rage and your jaw clenches up and all you can think is where's the head that this headstone is for and all you can do is go directly off and find it. The last kind of headstone, the kind you find in graveyards, makes you feel a lot differently when you touch it. When you die they bury you in the ground and then put the headstone over where your head is now, six feet down and in a coffin, and they carve your name into the stone so that when people come to look for you they know where to find you. If it's a headstone belonging to somebody named WABASCH MANDICOT and you're playing hide-and-seek in the graveyard with a couple kids from the neighborhood because the construction site has a fence around it and you're crouching, winded, in the shade of the stone, winded from a run because Ned counted to ten way too fast, you'll feel the warm stone and the sharp carvings of engraved words against your cheek, which will be pressed against that stone in an effort to stay unseen. In that case the headstone would be warm and comforting and would make you giggle if you looked at the name carved into it, WABASCH MANDICOT, and your giggling would blow your cover. If, however, your uncle brings you to that same graveyard one day, out of the blue, and takes you to a headstone with the name SUZY TYCE carved into it and below that LEFT US ALL, ALL ALONE, TOO SOON, and your uncle says, "Here she is, son," though he is not actually your father, he's your father's brother, so you are not actually his son, your actual father is missing, perhaps he's alive on the moon or in a different country, just for sure not here beside you—beside you is a headstone that means your mother is below you. This headstone will be cold and covered in some invisible grit kicked up by a hard rain and that's basically how you'll feel, too, when you touch the carved letters of your weird last name.

HOMICIDE

You have no part in the deal of your own death. The death of other living things, on the other hand, is a different matter. You can kill other living things. You can also kill yourself, but if you did that you would lose the opportunity to kill in the future. Killing is best done with sharpened sticks, headstones, knives, or guns. Knives and guns can be hard to come by, but if you have one knife, you have spears for life. There's no feeling like the feeling you get when you've sharpened spears all day in your treehouse and then you look down at the pile of sharpened spears. It's bad manners of the worst kind to kill innocent beasts of the woods and ponds, though many children are drawn to this type of killing. The only types of justifiable killings are self-defense and revenge killings. If a pack of four boys surrounds you as you make your way home from a tree fort in the woods when no one else is around, and these boys pin you to the ground right on top of a rock that feels like it's punching a hole in your back and then they rub leaves covered in dog shit on you, punch you ten times and run away, you'll feel the need to kill one or more of these boys. The first thing you do when you pull yourself up off the ground is look around for any nearby head-stones. You will be doing some quick archaeology. A good headstone will settle the score right there and then, and you won't have to plan a revenge killing for later. Just wait for the group to split up, and use the headstones on the one who did you the worst. Aim for his eye. Your aim will be good because you have homicide on the mind. Get the others back, too, one by one, over time. In the movies they never go for the worst guy first, which works to your advantage in real life, because the worst guy will expect you to go for one of his minions before you go for him, but he will be wrong.

INCEST

Cousins, the children of your aunt or uncle, are sexually off-limits as far as modern middle- and upper-class Americans are concerned. I mention this only because of the times I'd be standing on the porch of my uncle's mansion when he was having a cookout, and a bunch of adults would be milling around drinking beer and pre-paring fireworks when one of them would say, "Hey, look over there," and point to the place on the horizon with the trailer and the black smoke curling into the sky, where people were loitering in the yard working on a car or chasing off a dog, and then the person who spoke would comment that "those people probably have sex with their cousins." At times like this, if Isabella was around, I'd blush and run down to the basement.

ISABELLA

The daughter of my uncle, six years my senior, avid equestrian, weekly visitor to the mansion, one time took me to the movies. She was my first true love. Isabella was also among my uncle's greatest loves, though I loved her more than he did. Or maybe he loved her as much as I did but he just didn't know how to show it. He loved his bugle. He showed that by playing it so beautifully. I showed Isabella I loved her by hanging up her parka on the hall tree when she visited in winter, by bringing her popsicles when she visited in the summer, and by tidying things up in the kitchen when I heard she was coming over. I'd mow the lawn for her, clean the mold off of her purple folding chair and place it in her favorite spot so when she came she could just lie out and relax. Things took a turn for the worse when she left for France and met the astronaut. The time I knew Isabella the least, when we were light-years apart, was on the day of her wedding. I will never forget it. My aunt had been dead for years, but my uncle had commissioned a bust of her and had placed it at the head of one of the long tables that had been set up in the yard. Dinner came, then cake. Isabella and the astronaut kissed. My uncle gave a bugle solo, lit off a huge firework, and then five gypsies in white tuxedos tore the linen coverings from a new wing of the mansion: a huge bedroom with a private entrance, a blue-painted nursery for the grandchildren, and a bathroom with a hot tub. I was in the highest limb of the sycamore tree in the yard of the double-wide trailer, spying with binoculars through the clouds of smoke that rose from tires in the campfire. A little girl at one of the long tables let go of a red balloon she was holding and shrieked as it flew away. I wished, on the balloon, that the marriage would not last, and it didn't. A month later, Isabella left the astronaut to explore her inner self in Mexico City, and he showed up at my uncle's house in a car filled with vacuum-packed clothing and gear, sat down at the kitchen table, and revealed the fact that he'd been sterilized by a NASA experiment gone wrong. He went on to say that Isabella wasn't interested in kids anyway, nor in fact was she interested in him.

INDEX

Not THE index, just AN index, unalphabetized, of entries I am still researching:

Light, Lit, Aflame, Amok, Kindle, Air Show, Instinct, Attack, Sugar Rots Teeth, Jelly-Bean Alchemy, Mezzo-soprano, Kale, The Sharpening of Spears, Caring for Your

Rattlesnake, False Bite, Mysterious Charges, Phony, Dent Repair Tool Kit, Hail Ice Cream, El Hondero's Big Balloon Repair, Divine Intervention, Papal Hallucinations, Gold Nipple Piercings, Cabbage, Dental Emergencies, Going Shoeless, Depression, The Use of Fish as Bait, Pigs, Pig-Hair Coat, Triangulation, Disorientation at Sea, REM Sleep to Waking Transitions, Ball Pit, Nudity and Cake, Escalators, Scarecrows.

ICING OF CAKE
Most arousing part of a cake. Inexplicably most arousing in white. Also known as frosting. Eating of the icing is forbidden before the cake has been revealed. A week following her marriage, in the middle of the night, Isabella ate icing from the leftover cake, standing by the fridge, in the yellow light, alone, sucking it from her finger. I saw it all from the top of the stairs.

JELLY FLYTRAP
Jelly is a gelatinous substance resulting from the super-heating of ripe fruit and sugar. Jelly is stored in glass jars in pantries. Pantries are a great place to hide if you're trying to eavesdrop on important conversations held in kitchens, especially if there are a bunch of aprons for you to hide behind. You can get jelly to hang off the edge of a piece of bread if you put enough on. Tilt the bread and

watch the jelly defy gravity. Put more and more jelly on the bread until you have a jelly mountain. Put the jelly mountain outside your window, then bring it in after a while and it will have flies stuck on it. Pick the flies off and feed them to your Betta Fish as a treat.

JOURNEY INTO DEEP SPACE

Start on Earth, go up. You're in the clouds, and up: thinner clouds, freezing air, the upper edge of the atmosphere. Now you're seeing ice crystals and other, more mysterious forms of water hanging suspended above the land. Go up a little more and you enter the vacuum of space. Earth curves away from you, blue and egg-like. Keep going up (though the idea of UP is, by the time you're here, nonsense) until Earth is a pinprick in the distance, the sun a glowing marble, and stop—you're on the cusp of deep space. Deep space doesn't have depth like a pool does. Deep space has neither surface nor bottom. It is at this moment, when the sun is a marble reflecting in his visor and Earth is a tiny blue point, that the astronaut is on the cusp of deep space. On the cusp of deep space he feels more alone than ever, more alone than he did the day Isabella left, more alone than he will ever feel again. When he looks into deep space he sees an endless swarm of amoebas and whirlpools, huge orbs of light pulled like melted cheese from the lips of black holes, endless mysteries of which he could become a part, and that's when the loneliness really hits him, when his loneliness is the loneliness of the dead. He must only adopt the identity of memory itself, must understand that he will exist as memory while existing, still, as a flesh-and-blood human, to let the bow of his ship pass silently across the threshold.

JUTE AND ALABASTER

Alabaster is a white, bone-like material whose origins are unknown. Some say it just washes up onshore one day and that you find it among the stones on the beach. Others say alabaster is expelled once every four years, on a full moon in spring, from the beak of a falcon. Alabaster was what El Hondero used to prove his identity the day he showed up at the door of the parachute house, after the hail came through the material, the first time I met him. Tucking a wad of dense black curls above his ear, he revealed what hung from its lobe: whittled in alabaster, hanging on a brown string of tightly wound plant fiber known as jute, there was a rendition of lightning striking an arrow in flight.

KERNELS OF THE PAST

Memories are stories like little chunks of jute with two fraying ends. The more you handle the jute, the more it falls apart. A bit of frayed rope: your parents on a bus that's overgrown with weeds, little piles of dirt in the aisle inside the bus, your mother sweeping, telling you not to step in the piles. Nothing more before or after that memory. No ropes leading anywhere from there. Just more frayed bits you catch the same way you catch tiny things that stick to your feet after you've walked barefoot across a carpet. Why do you remember, all of a sudden, licking your mother's neck as she carried you, and that her skin tasted like bananas? How could you have known what a banana tasted like? And, most bizarrely: How can you miss something you can't remember losing? Another lost memory: the sound of a cry somewhere above my head, I look up, then the sight of a moving black shape, the black shape of a boy falling from the limb of a tree, the black shape taking up more and more of my vision— then the impact. Why do I only remember it now: the trauma, the breathless panting in the grass, the grass in my mouth, blades of it on my tongue, the feeling of suffocation . . . Another chunk of frayed rope with no use. There was a month of my life during which I was sure that I'd been struck by lightning as a child and that I'd only just remembered it, but then I realized there was no way of knowing for sure and there was nothing I could do about it, anyway.

KINETICS

Kinetics is the physics of moving. The science of kinetics is what you have to explain to everyone when they ask why it is that they launch farther off the trampoline when they're jumping alongside heavy-set children. I don't think it was a boy falling from the limb of a tree. It was a boy launched high into the air by the force of a trampoline, and the boy was Ned. It must have been Ned's house I was at because Ned was the one person I knew who owned a trampoline. I remember I lay there in the grass beside the trampoline with the wind knocked out of me, thinking I was dying. Ned's mom called my uncle's mansion and then Isabella came to pick me up. My wind came back quickly, and I was better by the time Isabella came, and I could have stayed, but I left with her anyway. I told her I thought I'd been struck by lightning and she said, "When, now?" "Back when I was little," I said. She said that might explain some things about me. Then she said I probably shouldn't go to the doctor because what would he be able to do about it, un-strike me? Plus I was alright the way I was. She pulled on my hair and said that if I'd been struck by lightning my hair would come out very easily and that it didn't so that proved I hadn't been struck. I told her to let go and she let go, but then I wanted her hand back on my head. She dropped me off at my uncle's, then drove off without saying goodbye. The next day I saw Ned walking around with some boys from the Crushers. Things had gone kinetic.

KNEE-HIGH SOCKS

Physical education, or P.E., holds all the fun of Little League, but lost in a sea of social politics, terrible body-consciousness, and constantly shifting, ambiguous rules. With few exceptions, a schoolboy will find himself forced to attend P.E. most frequently during the series of months when his body is most severely in flux. At the height of puberty, schoolchildren are forced to strip down to loose shorts and knee-high socks and then to lift weights before an audience of their peers. A boy in knee-high socks might be assigned to spot you while you lift weights, but his spotting will involve talking about taking showers with girls and will have nothing to do with making sure you don't drop the weights. If you get tired of his story, drop one on purpose.

KEEPING SCORE

Gambling is staking one thing on another thing, the first thing being a for-sure thing, and the second thing being theoretical. The idea behind gambling is best illustrated with an example. Let's say you and your uncle are in the unfinished basement, kneeling on the concrete floor eating popsicles while watching a cockroach and praying mantis battle to the death in a tank. It's dim down in the basement, but comfortable. Outside it's flaming hot. You broke a sweat trying to collect the roach and the mantis and you weren't about to watch the battle outside in the brutal sunlight. Beside the fish tank is a pile of one-dollar bills—some that are yours, some that came from your uncle. If the cockroach wins, the pile is yours. You gambled on the roach because he's bigger and he's faster but you know, in the back of your mind, that the serrated arms of the mantis are deadly to roaches. When you're older you keep gambling, only your odds get worse and the stakes get higher. You're getting in a car with strangers, spending whole weekends in abandoned Victorians in the park when you used to just run in, tag the attic window, and rush out. What once seemed like a bad idea might now seem like a good one. You will see no consequences where consequences clearly exist, and you will take on the debts that make you a true gambler.

LIFE OF GAMBLING

You use half-rotten timbers to build the floor of your tree-house: that's gambling with your life. You see a list of horse names and you bet the last of your money that one of those horses will pass the finish line before all the others: that's gambling with your finances. If a girl's parents don't want you going over to her house but you go over there anyway, and you go right around the time her parents are supposed to be getting home from work: that's gambling on the unlikely event that her parents will come home late or else get home on time but when they find you they will experience a sudden change of heart toward you. If the weather radar shows several big red blobs spinning toward Springfield and you and all the other gypsies pack your things and start driving there: that's gambling on hail. If you run out of money because you bet on the wrong horse and then you take out a loan against your house so that you can gamble some more: that's gambling with your shelter. If, later, after you've lost all the loan money and the creditors come knocking at your door, you set fire to that shelter on purpose so that you can collect the insurance money and leave town before the creditors find out about it: that's gambling with your freedom. The authority on high-stakes gambling is my uncle. To gamble is to lose, and he is an authority on loss, though he is far from the only authority on that subject.

LAWBREAKERS
People who are caught breaking the rules set forth by the authorities. The authorities believe that when you detain a man who has broken the law and you hold him in jail for some duration of time he will avoid engaging in the

kinds of activities in the future that would give them a reason to detain him again. If you impale someone on a spear, you'll probably go to jail for good. If you take three large balloons out for an unplanned flight and you lose control of them in gusty weather and they wind up causing a major traffic hazard (see BALLOONS) you're going to go to county jail for a month (see CALIBRATING THE BALLOONS). If you burn down your own house and the authorities find out about it, you go to federal prison and stay there for a lot longer than a month.

LIBRARY

A good place to go if you need to sit in peace and calmly think about what to do next, although it can also be a very difficult place to remain calm. If you're curious about something that happened in the past, say you're curious about why people lost interest in traveling by blimp and you don't know anyone you'd trust to provide facts about the decline of blimp travel, then you would go to the library, find a book about blimps, flip to the index and find POPULARITY, DECLINE OF, and you would go to the corresponding page. If you decided to read the whole book as a result of reading about the decline of the blimp, you'd take the book to the librarian, she'd check it out in your name, and you'd leave the library with it. The librarian's job is not just to check out books. It is also to make sure that nobody does anything crazy in the library, that everyone stays quiet so that people reading can think, and that everybody gets a turn on the computer. The library is supposed to be a place of peace and quiet, but it can very quickly become very exciting. I once saw El Hondero run full-tilt through the library doors with a book he hadn't checked out. That was back before I knew who he was. Another time, after I'd met him, El Hondero tore up a library book that had reproductions of photographs in it. I know this because he gave me a photograph he'd torn from a book. The paper was glossy with one ragged edge, and in the picture an old man stood on the deck of a houseboat that was tied up on the banks of a wide, muddy river. The river was light brown and the man in the picture was just lighter than the river—he looked like he came out of that river as a baby and had lived on it since. Beneath the photograph was a caption that read JIM 'RIVER' SWIFT BESIDE HIS BOAT—PHOTO BY HOWARD TYCE, and beneath the caption were words that El Hondero had written in red ink: YOUR LAST NAME? PHOTOGRAPHER YOUR RELATIVE? THIS TAKEN DOWNSTREAM 100 MILES—SEE BRIDGE. In the corner of the photo was a unique-looking bridge suspended by wires that stretched from two towers, one on each bank. That's how I came to suspect that my dad was alive, down the river somewhere, and that his real name was Howard. HOWARD, at the time, sounded something like an Indian name, and I thought that would make some sense. The one time my uncle said his name, the name he said was RAY. There were times I cared and times I didn't care what my dad's real name was, or that my dad could have been alive somewhere. Around the time El Hondero gave me the torn-out picture by Howard Tyce I was frying other fish: I was figuring out a routine that did not involve my uncle.

LIBRARY LISTS

The library is full of lists. There's a list for who goes next on the computer, a list of people who aren't allowed back, a list of books that are good for people mourning the loss of a loved one, and a list of numbers you can call if you suspect bad things are happening to somebody you know. Then there's the genealogy section. A librarian named Denise introduced me to the genealogy section—her favorite place in the library—and for a day, the section kept me interested. The genealogy section was really just a thousand books of lists. Denise showed me how to find my mother's name in the huge genealogy books. It turns out that my mother was called Suzy Paciano before she was called Suzy Tyce, which made perfect sense. PACIANO sounded to me like a type of bean, and TYCE I had always thought of as a botanical concept—a shoot, maybe. Suzy Paciano became Suzy Tyce a year before the day I was born, and Suzy Tyce was listed as deceased a few years later. I had no memory of this, so I must still have been a baby. According to the genealogy book, Suzy Tyce had died at an Institution for the Insane. Denise put her hand on my shoulder when we read that part together, but I wasn't exactly sad. I'd seen my mother's headstone. The name of the place where she lived when she died, PARTING WATERS, was what I was most interested in. PARTING WATERS sounded like a place that was floating, and living on the water sounded good. PARTING WATERS made me picture an enormous ark but for the insane instead of animals. When we looked for Howard Tyce, we found only my dad's dad's name, Ebenezer Tyce, and we found neither my uncle nor my father, but Paciano could not have become Tyce by itself, and so I realized that the genealogy books were flawed, falla-cious, and boring.

No matter how badly you want to do it, you must not give in to the burning need to rearrange books the way you think they should go. Do not rearrange the books. Do not rearrange the books. There is no better system than the alphabetical one, although it is not a good system. There is no better system than the Dewey Decimal, although that is an even worse system.

My father took photographs of people who lived on a river near a hanging bridge somewhere, and that's all I knew.

LIVING IN BUNKHOUSES FOR GIRLS AND BOYS WHO ARE WARDS OF THE STATE

If you're left with no place to stay because, for instance, the place where you were staying was burned down, your uncle is in jail, you're left with no money, and you're still technically a minor, the state is obliged to deal with you. This is a situation you do not want to end up in. How the state deals with you is they put you in a bunkhouse. A bunkhouse is a place where you live in a huge room with lots of other people in the same situation as you, a place where you spend your days waiting around for meals, the occasional math class, or one of the many TRAINING OPPORTUNITIES provided by businesses in the area who want cheap, unskilled workers. Most of these bunkhouses provide easy opportunities for escape and reentry, so the industrious orphan is able to adopt side projects and build himself an alternative plan. Most of the nights you spend in a bunkhouse are very uncomfortable. There are bugs, people snore, people sleepwalk or just regular walk, people touch you, there are fights, if you're thirsty you have to wait until the morning to get water, the bedding is itchy, you overhear strange things, you see ghosts, it's always steaming hot or freezing cold, the beds are hard, and someone named Fred won't leave you alone until you look at his magazines. The only time a bunkhouse is bearable, when it's actually borderline enjoyable, is when it storms hard outside. The roof of a bunkhouse is tin, and so when it storms you close your eyes, listen to the sheets of rain on the tin, feel stray drops hit your face, and sleep the whole night through.

LIFTING BRIDGES

A lifting bridge is a special kind of bridge that is fitted with huge pulleys and counterweights that move the road up and down when tall boats need to pass beneath. I learned all about the different types of bridges and why they looked how they did when I finally tried, one day, to locate the bridge in the torn-out photo by Howard Tyce. The bridge in the picture, it turned out, was a common type of bridge found all around the country, and so I was stuck. I wasn't able to narrow it down to less than maybe fifty different bridges. It happened that, around the same time as I was learning about which bridges were on what river, I was also hanging out beneath a bridge near the bunkhouse pretty regularly. All bridges serve functions their builders did not intend: a roost for birds, a place from which to jump to your death, and a place to test your echo—though that's not all of them. If you've escaped your bunkhouse and you want to drink a lot of beer, a great place to go is under an old lifting bridge on the banks of a river. It's fun to watch the things that float by in the muddy water, it's fun to listen to the sounds of birds and cars passing high above you while you drink, and it's fun because you know nobody will care if you fall asleep on a rock there.

LIGHT-UP WATCH

A watch with a time you can read at night because it has a button you press that makes the little screen light up green. You have light-up shoes, light-up necklaces, and then you have your light-up watch. All of them light up but only one is truly useful. El Hondero gave me a plastic Casio with a calculator function and a light-up display. It was waterproof to a hundred meters and told the time in twenty-four or twelve. That watch was the best thing that anybody had ever given me.

LIMBER

Agile, bendable, spry, the opposite of stiff. The word LIMBER probably comes from someone with the ability to vault from tree limb to tree limb. Climbing ladders is only for the limber. Children are far more limber than adults, with a few exceptions. My uncle once tried to get into my treehouse through the trapdoor but could not, and he never tried again. He was not a limber man.

Slipping your body through gaps in the teeth of huge cogs in the engine room of a huge, rusting machine that years ago would lift and lower the center section of a bridge: that's only for the limber. El Hondero was a very limber man. He had what he called dexterity, and said he'd gotten it from his summers working as a corn de-tassler in Iowa. He was up the rusty ladder in a flash and climbed around on the metal bridge like a chimpanzee. I moved like a sloth compared to him, and I was no amateur. I'd been limbered by the time I'd spent in trees and I had courage I'd gained in their canopies, but the bridge was a different story. El Hondero was through the engine room and out the tiny hatch on the far side before I'd made it between the first set of pistons. When I at last came sliding through the hatch into daylight, I found him sitting at a little classroom desk on the platform above the river. It was as if he'd been there all along, quietly reading and sipping broth from the bowl he held in his hands, dribbling broth across the book that was open on the desk in front of him.

LIFE IN RUNOFF

When rain falls from the sky, hits the earth, and keeps moving, it becomes runoff. Drips of rain from eaves, technically, are runoff. Probably not for long, since they usually fall on dirt and sink in. In some cases, buildings are built so close together that rain flows a long way before it disappears into a creek or gets soaked up by the earth. This was how it was at the Wilson Carmichael Bunkhouse for Boys and Girls: ten squat buildings housed two hundred wards of the state, and between these metal-roofed buildings was a concrete sidewalk. When it rained hard, the runoff traveled downhill to the southeast corner of the compound, through a rusted culvert, beneath a gravel road, across a steep hillside of shifting granite boulders, and finally into the algaed face of a black-water pond overgrown by immense oak and cedar trees and bordered by wild, yellow-blooming lilies. It's been said that prisoners love the feeling of rain on their faces. Same goes if you feel trapped in your body: you may find yourself looking into the clouds as they rain on you. You may wish you could do as rain does and transpire. You may look into the algaed face of a black-water pond and wonder how you'd feel as a part of that water, or at the bottom of it, under a rock.

LOOT

At the bottom of the ocean, behind an enormous granite boulder, in a cave full of eels and enormous crabs, lies Blackbeard. If you can get there he's yours and so is his loot, though technically it still belongs to whoever it was that Blackbeard killed for it. When you come upon ancient treasure you either sell it on the streets or you sell it to a museum. Either way, someone's going to profit, so it might as well be you. Take what loot you find. Children are trained from a very young age to be looters—think of the jelly beans and chocolate eggs at Easter. If you find the metal door to the bunkhouse cafeteria has been left open by the kitchen staff, loot swiftly. Take only your portion—what you'd eat over a month, for example—and find a good place to hide it so that your loot won't itself be looted. All archaeologists are looters, it's just that some have a museum to back them up. El Hondero had an Indian pot made a thousand years ago and this pot he used as a tip jar when he played gypsy-fiddle downtown—this old clay pot, which was painted with a pattern of black-on-white triangular spirals, got a lot more attention than it would have in a museum. El Hondero sometimes sold things to pawnshops and flea markets, too, but only to people who he thought knew how to treat an artifact with respect.

LILIES AND SNAPPING TURTLES
Clear evidence that dinosaurs are not entirely extinct, the mature snapping turtle is better armored than a truck tire and has a beak that can rip through a bicep. It has a piercing scream that can only be heard, underwater, by other turtles. A snapping turtle spends its time paddling

the muddy currents of ponds and rivers with its webbed feet, waiting on the bottom and holding perfectly still, beak open, its pink, wormlike tongue squirming in such a way that fish come by to eat the worm and are snapped up before they know it. While I was staying at the Wilson Carmichael house, I once found a baby snapping turtle beneath a bridge, collected it, and kept it in a box beneath my bunk. I thought I'd heard somewhere that snapping turtles liked to eat lilies so I went to the pond and got some yellow lilies for him but he wouldn't eat them and they wilted in his shoebox. Then I tried feeding him some copper wire and he ate that. I tried dead frogs and he ate those, too.

LOOKING FOR GHOSTS

A ghost is an energetic manifestation that can be perceived by conscious humans but cannot be explained by physics. People usually perceive ghosts when they're between sleep and waking. The more we know about them, the more ghosts seem to be projections of the mind onto reality rather than vice versa. Traditionally, a ghost was imagined to be the soul of a dead person. I would say that a ghost is the projection of a memory of a person or other sentient thing, a projection so powerful that the mind cannot see itself as its source. It isn't unusual for a person to experience a finite period of ghost-vision. Lots of people have awoken one day with an ability to perceive ghosts and then lost that ability a week or so later. Often, the ability to see ghosts comes to you during times of difficulty. The ghosts I saw during my time in the bunkhouse were the ghosts of other teenagers: dead boys and girls who had used my bunk before me and just wanted to lie down.

LOCOMOTORY OPTIONS USED BY TEENS WHO ARE WARDS OF THE STATE

If he isn't getting around on his own (using roller skates, bicycle, canoe, borrowed scooter), a teenage ward of the state is subjected to regular, involuntary shipment to and from a charter school in a dented blue van driven by an alcoholic named Charlie.

LOWRIDER DX-1

The name of the bicycle I'd ride in the days of the bunkhouse, the LowRider was built as a hybrid mountain/ BMX bike. LowRiders came in purple, red, silver, and black, but mine I'd spray-painted green-and-brown camo so I could easily ditch it in the weeds and not have it get stolen. The LowRider DX-1 had three gears you shifted by twisting a rubber grip on the handlebars. Its wheels were fat and had deep treads. The LowRider DX-1 was marketed to teenagers and came, if you bought

it new, with a book of advice written by a famous mountain biker. If you couldn't afford to buy a LowRider new,
you could check around at pawnshops or find a kid who
had one but didn't ride it and then trade him something
for it. The first generation of LowRider owners didn't
generally keep their bikes for very long. The first generation of LowRider owners was quickly unseated by the
second generation of LowRider owners. If you were a
rich kid who got a new bike every few months and went
out for a ride by yourself the day after you got your new
LowRider, and let's say you stopped to take a look at the
useless advice manual that came with the bike a mile or
so into your ride, on a path that led through a city park,
that's when you'd be likely to encounter a soon-to-be
second-generation LowRider owner: usually a shirtless
boy whose ribs you could see through his skin, whose
skinny arms showed muscles like lemons when he flexed
them, who could, if he wanted, unseat you from the
LowRider with a palm-sized headstone thrown from ten
yards out but who would, if you were lucky, first ask
nicely.

LOSS OF TRACTION
Let's imagine a blacktop running through the country on
a warm afternoon in late spring. The road has its hills
and curves, it passes through forests and fields. Imagine

a red sedan with its windows down proceeding along the road at a moderate pace—let's say the driver is Patty, for example (see COURT ORDER), and you're watching her from the ditch on the side of the road, where you've jumped with your LowRider because you glimpsed her car from a distance—the red sedan, in this case, is not likely to lose traction, though you may in your mind be imagining the car losing traction and smiling to yourself as you think about it. But no, she takes the turns carefully. All of her tires remain on the road. She could drive under these conditions and not lose control. She has a distinct purpose and is advancing toward her goal at a cool forty miles per hour with no loss of traction. Let's compare Patty's progress down the blacktop with your own progress down a gravel road at the edge of a forest, with a field on your left and the forest on your right, in a hard late-summer rain. The sky is a graphite background across which cream-colored, smokelike clouds are rushing right to left, and the rain is coming down in sheets. You're on your LowRider DX-1 painted the colors of camo and you're soaked to the core, clothes like a sponge and boots little aquariums, and you're pedaling hard on the bike and laughing aloud, spitting up rainwater, blinking to clear your rain-filled eyes, laughing because you've looked out across the field at the sheets of rain, one after the other bending the young corn and pattering a billion drops against the broad green leaves, and you've been hit with a sense of being alive. In minutes you'll be back at the bunkhouse, you'll be met by the warden and be punished or be told to stay out, but you're not thinking about that right now. It's you and your bike and you're about to cross the creek, flowing through the woods to your right, swollen with runoff, its banks shedding mud and shucking out rocks, and then there's a crunching sound like a mouthful of cornflakes and you're on the ground. You're resting with your cheek on the gravel and can see a thousand tiny rivers flowing through the gravel that looks like boulders from this close. You throw the LowRider into the woods once you've gotten up on your feet, and you limp onward through the rain. Then, when you look back to mark in your mind the spot where you ditched the bike you see, straddling a bike of his own, stopped in the middle of the gravel path maybe a hundred yards from where you're standing, an adult. You can't see his face and don't recognize his body. You feel hot blood running down your forearm from a cut on your elbow. Then he gets up on his bike and goes back the way he came, slowly, looking once over his shoulder before he vanishes in the rain.

LOCKED OUT

In the middle of the night, the doorbell rings. You wake up and go to your uncle's room and he's not there. The doorbell rings again and you walk down the stairs, in the dark, to the front door. You open it and there's your uncle sitting down on the front steps. Somehow he's lost his keys between the car and the front door, and he's locked out. Months later, after your uncle's been locked up, on a rainy day when you've limped back to the bunkhouse after an unfortunate loss of traction, you find the gate locked. You're wet and angry but you have a few dollars so you go to the gas station, go around back to the dumpsters, and find a guy who will buy you beer. It's a full moon and the clouds are gone and you limp down to the lifting bridge and sit down on a rock beneath it and you drink the beer.

LETTERS READ IN PRIVATE

A letter is a symbol, no more alive than a stone, that is arranged among other letters in such a way that the combination comes alive. If someone says, "You got a letter," though, he'll be referring to the other kind of letter, the kind you get in the mail, the kind printed on white, semi-transparent paper that's come from a stinking pulp mill on the banks of a river somewhere. When you hold a sheet of letter paper up to the light and look past the words, you can see that the whiteness, which from a distance looks uniform, now has blotches of light and dark within it. These blotches of light and dark in the sheet of paper are like a sky socked in with cloud or a fog-covered river you're looking down on from a bridge. If you receive a letter that's been sent specifically to you, odds are it contains some information you might find important. Let's say you're living as a ward of the state in a bunkhouse. You're wearing the same set of clothes as everyone else and you have a number assigned to you that people use in place of your name. And let's say that one day, out of the blue, you get a letter with your name on it, a letter which is brought to you by one of the court-ordered types who up to that point had no idea who you are. You'll clutch this letter with all the strength you have and retreat with it to a place where there's no wind to steal your letter and no strangers to pester you as you read or take your letter away. You'll get in your bunk and pull the yellowish-white bedsheet up over your head like a tent. In that small, private space, the most private space you can find, you'll read the letter, and reading it will take you even deeper, into an even more private space that's beyond the earth altogether.

LOOSE MEATS: SALISBURY STEAK
A sick joke, Salisbury Steak is served on special occasions at publicly funded institutions such as jails and bunkhouses. Salisbury Steak is not a steak at all but is in fact a crude loaf made from red-stained bits of discarded meat. Salisbury Steak can be cut with the thumb as if the thumb

were a knife. Consuming Salisbury Steak leads to extreme indigestion and difficulty breathing. Salisbury Steak is either completely bland or salted to a point where it could be classified as toxic, and is served beneath a brown slurry that develops a reflective skin at room temperature.

LUMINESCENCE

Nothing glows on its own. A thing that glows is burning energy from the sun that it has locked up inside. The moon's light, on the other hand, is a reflection. Insects that glow green in the night glow on sunlight held captive the way fire burns on dried wood—everything luminescent is feeding on the sun. To glow, you need fuel. You need to eat. Anything that glows in the darkness of the night is called LUMINESCENT. This I learned late one night beside the runoff pond with a girl, Michelle, who lived at the bunkhouse. She pointed to the green glow emanating from the pond and said it was called LUMINESCENCE. A person's skin can also seem to glow, and you may want to be inside of it. Sometimes you may want to have another person's skin surround you like the walls of a parachute house. Feelings can also be luminescent—physical sensations experienced in the darkness can glow with warm heat and then disappear all of a sudden as if obscured by a cloud.

LONELY

It's about as possible to talk about what it means to be lonely as it is to talk about what it means to be happy, sad, or content. To say, for example, that being lonely involves actually being alone would be fallacious. I can only make guesses about what I, for some reason, remember as having been a lonely moment. The lonely moment may not have been, itself, lonely. It may be the memory recalled after the fact—the consequence of reliving a memory through remembering it—that is evoking something like loneliness. It's possible that my loneliest time was that night I slept at Ned's, but I can't really know. Ned wasn't even there at the time. My uncle dropped me off at Ned's and said Ned's mom would be expecting me. I say I was lonely in retrospect partly because Ned wasn't there—he was sleeping at a friend's place—and because while I lay there in Ned's bed, listening to the crickets, my uncle was burning down his mansion. At the time, was I lonely? I might have been content, lying there in the dark, listening to Ned's mom and dad whispering to each other in the next room. I only knew what had really happened the next day, after the fact.

"MANO-A-MANO": WHAT IT MEANS TO "HAVE A TALK"

When someone tells you "we need to have a talk," you can be sure that trouble is on the horizon. If the person telling you had something simple to say he would have just said it to you rather than alert you to the fact that he plans on saying it to you in the future. Most times, "the talk" will occur in the office of the person who requested the talk. Sometimes when you go into the office you will find just the principal, other times you will find a group of official-looking people who stop talking when they see you and who pretend they're happy to see that you've shown up. "The talk" will be a one-sided affair, though they will pretend to care about your opinion. They will not, in fact, need to talk with you about anything because they've already decided something, something big, and they're telling it to you because it has to do with you and your future. Sometimes the initial talk you are forced to have will not involve expulsion, termination, or imprisonment, but you can be sure that the third talk with the same officials will result in an irreversible change of life for you. For example, let's say you are told by the principal at your school or the warden at your bunkhouse that you need to have a talk, and when you go into his office he says, "Did you put a snapping turtle in Ernesto's bed?" you are not, in fact, being asked a question. You might well say, "I was there when the turtle was placed in Ernesto's bed, but I was only there because I was trying to stop Sasquatch from placing the snapping turtle, which

Sasquatch had found in a drainage ditch, in Ernesto's bed," but it won't matter because you'll be deemed incorrigibly delinquent anyway and expelled from the bunkhouse. Don't even try asking "Where am I supposed to go?" because those doing the talking will either have no idea where you're supposed to go, or they will have a plan for you and that plan will stink.

MATING
What animals do in order to make more of themselves. Mating refers to the animal sex act, but not to the sex act between humans. Different animals mate in different ways, but usually the mating act involves a male animal stacking itself on top of a female, rubbing its body against the body of the female, and releasing the fluid sperm which mixes with gelatinous eggs that the female has produced. If you're interested in beholding the act of mating I suggest you find the nearest body of stagnant freshwater that's shaded by trees and not often visited. You'll know you're on the right track if the ground begins to slope downward and the undergrowth begins to thicken. As you near the place of mating, you'll start to smell the plants rotting in the stagnant water and you'll start to hear the sounds of the animals mating. The best mating ponds have a green skin through which leaping frogs will pierce holes when you near the bank. PLOP,

PLOP, PLOP, you'll hear as you near the pond, and you'll see the green skin healing where the frogs went in. When frogs mate, a frog wraps its arms around a bigger frog and the two float around, embracing like this, all night long in the mating pond. The word for the mating position of frogs is AMPLEXUS, and it's as peaceful as it sounds. After they've floated around for a while in amplexus, the bigger frog, the female, releases a thousand little eggs, which the smaller frog, the male, feels sliding out beneath him. That's when he releases his sperm, which fertilizes the eggs, and then the eggs sink to the bottom of the pond or tuck themselves between stones where they wait to become tadpoles. When stray cats mate at the mating pond it's a much less peaceful experience and it happens inside the dripping culvert that feeds the pond with runoff. There is nothing luminescent about the sex acts of other animals. Nobody knows why animals mate in such dark and secret places, but it's probably born from a desire to be alone. Dogs, however, are an exception, and they love to mate in public. It's possible they do this because they enjoy being squirted with water hoses in the act.

MEETING FORTUITOUSLY
Meeting fortuitously is a thing that happens and results in a good outcome you didn't anticipate. Say you're drunk

beneath a bridge, alone, and you've decided to get into a stinking, flooded river just to see where it takes you, and a figure from your past appears and advises you not to carry out your plan: this is meeting fortuitously.

MOAT

A river that protects your fort. A good castle always has a good moat—one with hippos or alligators or huge snapping turtles in it. If enemies come to attack the castle all the king has to do is raise the drawbridge and let the animals do the work. El Hondero and I had a river protecting our platform under the bridge so technically it was a moat but it was a double-edged moat because if we weren't careful we'd roll off and fall into it while we were sleeping. One time one of the guys who hung around the library had a natural moat form around his fort after a hard rain. He told me that the moat was good for a while, that it was almost like magic because a thousand worms got pulled out of the earth and became a floating ball of worms in the water of the moat and he put the worms in a can and used them to catch fish later, but then the moat got too big and it washed away his tent fort and he had to climb up a tree for safety. In the letter I got from my uncle he wrote about a concrete moat that surrounded the jail he was living in. I wanted to see the moat, and I wanted to see my uncle, but his letter said he couldn't see me. I wanted to tell him that I wasn't mad at him anymore and that I hoped we could get another mansion together, one with a moat around it, so I sent him a letter back with a diagram of my dream mansion and numbers beside important elements of the mansion, the number one beside the turret, for instance, and included a glossary of the terms, but he must not have gotten my letter or else he didn't like it and tore it up.

MAN NAMED HANGING FROG

Hanging Frog was a Seminole Indian, and he was a prince in his tribe. One day, in his youth, colonists from Europe raided his village in the swamp and killed his whole family. Hanging Frog managed to escape by disappearing into the wilder parts of the swampy landscape, where no one alive had gone before. Three years later, on a hot day in the middle of the summer, three men commanding the force of raiding colonists sat swatting bugs off their skin and drinking rum right in the spot where Hanging Frog's village used to be. All around them were European-looking buildings and miserable white-skinned pioneers who had come to the swamp looking for gold. Right at the moment when the hot sun hung like a broiler in the center of the sky, Hanging Frog and five other Indians came silently across the swamp in a canoe and caught the heat-exhausted villagers by surprise. They scalped the colonists, each and every one, and lost none of their own party. Once they'd run what white men remained off the land, Hanging Frog returned, for a while, to his past habits of leisure. See MOONTAMING AND OTHER PEACETIME DEEDS OF HANGING FROG.

MOUND BUILDERS
One of the greatest of all mysteries is the mystery of the mounds. Everything I know about the mystery comes from El Hondero, author and metaphysician, hobo-archaeologist. He gave me a Casio watch and taught me how to catch squab. That watch, the clothes on my back, and my bookbag with some notebooks in it along with a set of Ned's clothes his mom had given me were about all I had left after the fire, but that was just about all I needed. El Hondero didn't have a lot more. He lived what he called a "Spartan existence," but his mind was always over-flowing. He would hold forth for hours about the mounds, and I would never tire of listening. Most people have heard something about a mound at one point or another: a finger pointing from the window of a moving car, a sign on the highway, the word MAN-MADE used in reference to the unremarkable spot of vaguely raised earth you're standing on . . . A few people have dug deeper into the evidence coming from the many tens of thousands of

mounds that dot the landscape of the United States (more in Canada, more still in Mexico). These researchers can be recognized by the way their eyes glow and their hands tremble when they speak on the subject. Some Appalachian tales hold that the Mound Builders themselves had eyes that glowed in the dark, eyes you can still see flashing today. And who knows? If you want to believe that the souls of ancient American builders of mounds carry on in the bodies of lightning bugs, that's your right and nobody can disagree with you. One of the thought exercises invented by El Hondero, which he guaranteed would allow you to enter a state in which the golden age of mounds could be lived in the mind's eye, went something like this: imagine you're standing on the top of a cliff over-looking a tree-filled valley stretching all the way to the horizon. Imagine you're so high up that you can see buz-zards floating the thermals below you. Now imagine that valley dotted with treeless hills rising high above the sur-rounding canopy like bubbles in a pot. Imagine all those painted or hide-covered people padding around their camps in the trees beneath the mounds or floating on a river so thick with fish they can catch them with bare hands. Imagine the bodies beneath the thatched roofs and the cloud of sweet smoke from an indoor fire, the barely audible sound of twigs crackling in the muffled light, the birds calling in the breezy canopy, and the mounds looming high and quiet over everything. This was how El Hondero told it to me, under the bridge on the night he came down to the river's edge after he'd spotted me wading into the current. Sometimes there were bodies of important people at the bottom of the mound, and sometimes the bodies were wearing jewelry made of something called mica which, when it's shaved thin, is translucent and luminescent. My mother, in her box beneath the earth, could have been wearing anything. She might have been covered in flowers or jewels when they closed the lid. I never thought to ask what she was wearing underground.

MEDICINE PEOPLE

You can't always heal by yourself. What if you start coughing one day and can't stop? If you live someplace cold and winter is coming on, you better hurry up and find yourself somebody with healing powers. This can get tough if you don't have money or anything else to trade. Modern America is a place where a boy with a bad cough and a fever, if he has no money, is basically the walking dead. Put it this way: there's a game going on and he's not allowed to play in it. If you find yourself in a situation like this, first try to relax and remember that many others have been here before you. Feel their hands on your shoulders in solidarity. Don't allow yourself to become overtaken by panic. Next you must rally yourself and stand up, walk down to the run-down part of town and find yourself someone who has healing powers. If you're lucky you'll happen upon a gypsy caravan or a gypsy parachute house. Once you're confident that you're in the presence of an actual folk healer, you must offer yourself up to her completely. You will know her by the pervasive sense of calm she seems to give off. Her voice will be soft. She will be dressed simply. When she touches you, and this is the biggest giveaway of all, you will feel a sensation of healing come through her hands.

MOLDING PAPER MATTRESS

A sleeping pad made from layers of pulp products such as newspaper, cardboard, and egg cartons, which has been left in a humid outdoor environment. To fall asleep on a molding paper mattress, try thinking of something good like the treasures deep in mounds. Picture the glowing mica schist. There are a thousand good thoughts that will lull you to sleep, but thinking about strange rocks seems to work very well. Picture weaving your way through all the razor-thin layers. Soon you'll be sleeping like the man with his mica, deep beneath the colored clay.

METHODS OF THE HUSTLE

A hustle is a way of making money without having a job. For fifteen-year-old orphans in the non-care of the government, the job market is severely limited. For some reason, people seem to hold it against the orphan that he is poor and parentless, and he's basically seen as a burden to everyone. People look at orphans and see future news headlines with the word MURDER in them. It's like the people around you are just waiting for you to freak out and start throwing things at the wall. It's different for baby orphans who are still cute and completely blank in the head—they have a chance of making it out of the whirl-pool. Either way, the good news is this: if you are particu-larly resourceful, have a little charisma, follow your own code of conduct, and have at least some training in things like common courtesy, empathy, and risks not worth taking, you probably have what it takes to become a great hustler. The classic hustle is the lemonade stand. A more advanced, more lucrative hustle is the collection of valuable metal and subsequent sale of the metal at a scrapyard. A subvariety of scrap-metal hustle: the slow progression of people silently walking up and down residential streets filling shopping carts with cans and then carefully inserting the sticky cans, one by one, into the crushing machine out-side the grocery store. While it's slow, tedious work, if you compare it to having a Daddy breathe down your neck while you drain hot grease from a deep fryer for five bucks an hour, scrapping cans is way better. The gypsies have a hundred hustles, one of which is hail-damage repair. Lots of people are doing the easy hustles like cans and the best hustlers are the only ones doing what they're doing, like for instance selling ancient mica artifacts on the black market. This was what El Hondero was doing when I met him, and he was pretty good at it, so good, in fact, that he needed a digging assistant on a mother lode of mica he knew about and asked me if I wanted to join in on his hustle when the time came.

MESH-BAG HUNTING

The act of catching pigeons by hand, often done on iron beams beneath bridges where pigeons doze in the hot summer sun. Down at your local Asian market is a guy or girl who has eaten pigeons before, knows how good they taste, and will buy the dead birds off you for at least a quarter a head. To be a successful squabbist, you need to not be afraid of heights and you need to be extremely limber. Here's what you do: First you wait until it's the hottest part of the day or the middle of the night. Then you climb up from beneath a tall bridge to the network of rafters and catwalks under the bridge. Be careful not to smack any of the rafters—they carry sound, and will scare off the birds. Even the slightest thump will ruin your squab hunt, so stealth is key. The upshot is squabs are dumb enough to return to that same rafter after they fly around for a while in a panic. Have a good-sized mesh bag on your hip when you go, and take your shoes off because, for one, bare feet are quiet and, for two, you get the best traction on the iron rafters—all that's keeping you from falling to your death while squabbing. NOTE: ENTRY IS UNFINISHED.

MOTHER LODE

A whole lot of something, usually something desirable like squabs or scrap metal or precious minerals, a mother lode is where you stock up. The mother lode of crushed beer cans is a tin mountain surrounded by barbed wire a mile or so down the river from El Hondero's bridge. Someday, in the distant future, someone will loot this mother lode for crushed cans he thinks are precious minerals. The mother lode of clues about my missing dad was the box of old photos I found beneath the enlarger in my uncle's basement, but the most important clue didn't come from the mother lode, it came from the book El Hondero found in the library, the photo that told us my dad was probably somewhere on this river, near that bridge in the photo, downstream.

MERKIN

Temporary wig used in the pubic area, popular among prostitutes, made of human hair or beaver pelts, often discarded in storm drains, sometimes used by squabs as material for their nests. It's hard to tell whether or not what you're dealing with is a merkin once it's spent some time exposed to weather. Could be any kind of hair. Could be a merkin. Could be a chunk of head wig. There is no market for the merkin or wig you find in a gutter or storm drain tangled up with sticks. The mother lode of merkin has to be in an osprey's nest atop a telephone pole or bridge strut.

MENTAL DADDY OF THE SELF: L'APPEL DU VIDE

Literally THE CALL OF THE VOID in French. Most definitions describe it as the feeling you get when you're standing on a high spot, so high it would kill you to jump, and when from nowhere you experience the nervous sensation that your body is about to actually jump itself off into the void, to its death, and you aren't going to be able to do anything about it. People will often grab hold of a nearby railing or get down on their bellies to widen the distance between possibility and reality—of course, there's nothing necessarily suicidal about the sensation of L'APPEL DU VIDE. It's a completely normal feeling and, ultimately, is a basic realization in your gut that you exist as a living human being, L'APPEL DU VIDE is an escape from the voice inside your head. L'APPEL DU VIDE is also a sign of the brain mechanism known as THE FREE WON'T. As far as D. D. Bayez, psychologist and author of several self-help books, is concerned, FREE WILL is either a complete myth or flimsier than a half-deflated balloon on a windy day. What actually drives decision-making is the FREE WON'T, the voice that says NO to the swarm of things you think about doing, the bad ideas that pass before the mind's eye at any given time. No, don't jump off the bridge. No, don't call your new friend a bad name for no reason and then spit on her in the middle of a perfectly enjoyable conversation, because doing this would be to jump your friendship into the void. Another example: once, El Hondero hired me to help him pour concrete. This was when he was working the concrete hustle, which was a two-part hustle, the first part being the excavation of the ground and looting of buried artifacts, the second part being the pouring of the concrete into a wooden form. On the day I worked with him it was brutally hot outside and El Hondero made me do all the digging so that he could have time to identify potential artifacts I'd dug up. All we found was an ancient axe-head made from chert. It didn't look like much to me, but El Hondero said it would fetch at least fifteen bucks on the black market. I mixed the concrete in a wheelbarrow as El Hondero polished the axe-head. Then I poured the concrete and El Hondero came over to smooth it as it poured. After he'd sculpted the quick-setting mixture so that it had a perfectly flat surface, just as he was skimming the last corner flat using a precise little spatula known as a trowel, I was overcome by the urge to create destruction. I took the shovel I was holding, brought it high above my head, and slapped the blade right into the middle of the setting slab. I instantly regretted it, and could hardly believe what I'd just done. El Hondero looked over at me, expressionless. I collapsed onto my knees and prepared for the consequences. We would have a talk, and then El Hondero would banish me from his life, I knew it. Instead what happened was that he pointed a finger at me—I will never forget this—he stood there, his fountain of black curls falling across the upper half of his body, his eyes covered by the dark sunglasses he wore most of the time, his tanned face slowly breaking into a smile and him saying, "The spirit of the wild slips through a chink in the wall." As it turned out, El Hondero knew exactly what had happened because he himself had been fighting the urge to destroy the perfect surface, and he knew that my wild outburst was a failure of the FREE WON'T, a victory of L'APPEL DU VIDE. I had heard the call and had answered it.

MOTH

Moths are nocturnal insects similar in many ways to butterflies, but very different. Their drab appearance is because light doesn't usually travel at night, so at night the eye can't see color. Moths have thick, soft scales which keep them warm as they fly through the night. It's been said that if a moth hits the proper light in the proper way, it can morph into a butterfly. A butterfly, on the other hand, can get bleached out and nocturnalized by a certain type of rare pollen that looks almost the same as the pollen butterflies spend all day poking around for in flowers. If their proboscis come in contact with the pollen which is not actually pollen as we know it, but a sort of crystallized moonbeam that has taken shelter from the sun beneath the petals of certain darkly colored flowers, then the butterfly will experience the total colonization of its body by moonlight and thus become a moth. Moths are like flying stones flaked very thinly. Their delicate, see-through wings are like mica. On a night when I was lonely and the rain had been coming down hard all day so I was bored and I couldn't sleep, El Hondero looked over from his book at the school desk and asked if I had a moment to assist with a midnight study he was about to undertake. Of course I agreed. It didn't matter what time it was. We got out a white bedsheet and a big flashlight and rigged the sheet between the rafters so the light would shine from behind it. In the space of an hour we'd collected eight different species of moth. El Hondero went along the sheet from moth to moth, looking at each with his magnifying glass, and I wrote down what he said: "Number four. Blue dot, each wing. Tiny head. No winglet. Salt-and-pepper thorax and straight, not curved, proboscis." At the end he said that each moth species represents a species of flower which is growing out there, and he gestured toward the curtain of rain. El Hondero never asked to see the catalog I was writing, and I never asked him why we'd done it. A study is a study and you shouldn't need a reason to do one.

MAKING THINGS UP

The Boy Scouts say you need food, water, and shelter to survive, but they forget to say you also need to make lists, and you need an imagination. With an imagination, you're never quite alone, even in a fort deep in the woods when nobody's around. Even when it's just you, you still have the ability to entertain yourself, which is important because otherwise your brain would turn to loam, like mud, when it should be more like mica schist. The moment Hanging Frog escaped from the murder and pillage of his village, he killed a fish, took it to a cave where it was safe and warm enough, and immediately named the cave HANGING FROG CAVE. He carved the image of a frog into the stone wall of the cave and made up a story of how he'd been saved by a huge bullfrog that came to him when he was floating through the swamp, set him on his back, and brought him to safety in the cave. He said the frog was wearing clothes like an Indian but was otherwise a frog so it seemed that the frog was a man who'd been transformed. Hanging Frog said, in his made-up story, that this frog-man hung from the ceiling in a little house that looked like a basket. You make things up whether you like it or not, same as when you breathe. When you're half-awake it's all you're doing. Putting two and two together so that they go.

MORE TYPES OF DREAMS

Flying dreams, naked dreams, chasing dreams where you're chasing, and chasing dreams where you're the one being chased, uncle-killing-you dreams, swimming dreams, dreams about people you used to see and never see anymore, dreams of your mother whom you've never known, dreams about the apocalypse, dreams about snakes, dreams about your cousin, dreams about sex that you wake up from wet, a dream where you're standing between two rotten trees in a traffic circle and a passing motorist tells you lightning is coming, you better move, but you can't, a dream where you're with your father on a houseboat in the river and the sun is setting through mica hands hanging on strings from the roof of the houseboat. Your father tells you to stand there, and you do, then he tells you don't stand THERE, stand HERE, and you do, then he starts to get frustrated but you don't know why until you realize he is trying to take your picture, which you realize because you've become him, you feel the camera in your hands and you see yourself, standing on the houseboat somewhere way downriver from the bridge where you're sleeping when you have this dream. In your dream, you see the bridge you've never seen in person, the bridge from the picture El Hondero tore out of a library book and gave you, except now it's a bridge made of gold beams hanging from gold cables, and then the dream ends with rushing water and a feeling of overwhelming dread.

MOONTAMING AND OTHER PEACEFUL DEEDS OF HANGING FROG

When Hanging Frog was a young man, he thought that the dreamworld was just as real as the waking one. Anything you saw while you were sleeping was meaningful, and dreams were often the result of your soul transporting itself temporarily into a different body someplace else. Hanging Frog, once he'd reclaimed his old village, went right back to his youthful habit of sleeping through the heat of the day, restlessly, always going from something resembling sleep to something resembling wakefulness, dreaming most of the time. Hanging Frog's vivid dreams were what led to most of his famous peaceful deeds, which are listed here:

- Making friends with the Medicine People of Many Cave Swamp
- Taming of the moon with the Mackinac Henge
- Discovery of the two child geniuses, killing of the evil child genius with a mica dagger
- Kicking down of the big dead tree and finding of the kingsnake inside
- Turning of the kingsnake into the Ohio River
- Construction of the lost Riverbank Earthworks

MORTAL BETRAYAL

This is when someone you trust does something hurtful to you and knows it. The worst kind of betrayal is when that someone who betrayed you shows no remorse or has disappeared entirely. Let's say you walk up to your fort in a tree in a city park, a fort you helped build—with your bare hands you pounded rusty nails into warped boards but still made it work, though it took you forever and it was freezing cold out when you built it—the same way you've walked up to it three times that week and you find that the ladder has been retracted from within. When you yell up there you hear someone say, "What's the password?" and it's your friend Michelle, who you'd brought to see the fort last week, and you say the password but a new voice from within the fort says the password is wrong, and it's the voice of a boy who a week earlier tried to beat you up and take your bike. In this situation you will feel the sharp sting of betrayal. Another example: your uncle burns down his mansion. Another example: you get kicked out of the bunkhouse, which is not at all betrayal because you never trusted the bunkhouse authorities in the first place, and before they can put into action their new plan for you that you know is going to stink you take everything you own (little bag of clothes, dictionary, letter from your uncle, plastic folder full of the most important lists) to the lifting bridge where your best friend lives. This best friend promises you a share in the mica expedition, provided you help him dig. This best friend gets your hopes up. He says you'd be living in a tent in the woods, that you'd get up at sunrise and dig in the mist, that you'd get to take breaks and go swimming in the afternoon. He says you'd make money. He says all you have to do is pay for a bus ticket to Ohio, and so you've saved up a hundred bucks over time selling squabs to the Asian grocery store. He tells you a lot of made-up stories and you believe them because that's what friends do. Imagine, then, climbing up the iron ladder beneath the bridge, limberly passing through the engine room singing to yourself, and arriving at the platform to find a note on the desk reading GONE TO OHIO. BACK IN A MONTH. And that's it. You're abandoned. So much for the mother lode of mica, if it ever even existed. Instead of all that you get a photograph your so-called friend tore out of a library book—a photograph taken by a guy who might possibly be your father—a father who, come to think of it, also betrayed you, unless he was abducted by aliens or mauled by a bear or was totally vaporized by lightning one day on his way to meet you. It's at this point you realize that nobody can betray you if you only rely on yourself.

MARITIME

This means time of the sea, as in not land time or air time or pond time, but ocean time. Maritime accidents are bad things that happen on the ocean. Maritime legends are stories that take place on the ocean. El Hondero made up a maritime story once, about how he was in the middle of the ocean and saw the first breath of a baby hurricane. He said that he saw these two gray clouds, not much bigger than people, floating right over the surface of the sea. He was fishing for skipjack in a canoe, he said, when he saw the two cloud people. The two gray cloud people noticed each other, started circling around one another like they were about to dance, then they came together and started whirling and sucking in all the other clouds around. El Hondero and I spent hours talking about his time on the ocean. We could talk for so long about the ocean in part, I think, because we knew that the softly gurgling water below us was flowing there.

MULLET

A mullet can be either a type of haircut or a fish. A mullet haircut is popular among gypsies, hockey players, hillbillies, and auto mechanics. The idea is that hair doesn't get in your eyes but is still long enough in the back so you can't get burned by the sun back there— though the truth is most people get mullets because they look cool. The fish known as mullet is a blunt-headed, blue-colored fish kind of like a catfish but that jumps out of the water a lot and lives mostly in the ocean, though I've seen mullet where there's no ocean nearby, and have in fact once caught a mullet in freshwater beneath a bridge near the Wilson Carmichael Bunkhouse, though people have called me a liar for saying so.

MYSTICAL VISION

A daydream of extreme power that has real-world meaning. You have your average daydreams and you have your mystical visions much the same as you have your minnow and you have your whale. In order to have a mystical vision, you must on some level be ready to receive it. You cannot receive a package without an address. You cannot get water from a tap unless you have a glass. Another thing: you cannot try to have a mystical vision. Mystical visions have you. El Hondero told me he'd had many visions. One led him to the burial mound of Hanging Frog, another to a storage unit containing ten thousand dollars' worth of rare porcelain dolls from Pakistan, and another to where at last we reunited, six months after he'd left for Ohio (see MORTAL BETRAYAL). For my part, I've had my own mystical visions, most notably while stalking squab in the rafters of the lifting bridge. In this vision I saw an old man walking through a curtain of vines and knew I was supposed to follow him and that was it—the whole vision. I had another, a longer one, where I floated like a huge balloon over everything and everyone for an entire day and saw everything clearly though nobody could see me. A mystical vision has on at least one occasion saved my life. You will know you are having a vision because it will feel like you've stepped through a portal into a different reality and what you find on the other side of that portal is a version of earth like earth but also not at all like earth. It's hard to describe, but you'll know it when it happens. When you realize it's happening, that you're having a vision, be ready to break into a dead sprint, get out of the water if you're swimming, or abandon your campsite in the middle of the night and strike out into the wilderness. Nobody knows where visions come from, or who sends them. When the vision comes, those questions won't matter, all that will matter is that you act—and act fast—since somewhere near you history is being written into past and you want to avoid being made a part of it.

MOMENT OF TRUTH

If you say that a moment is more true than another, you're saying that most moments are in some part false. When people say MOMENT OF TRUTH, they're not saying that they mostly live in a lie—they're using a figure of speech. The moment of truth is that moment when you decide to leap into the void beneath the bridge. It is that moment when you decide to push your raft out into the current of the river. The moment of truth is when you reach your arm right down in the catfish mud-hole. The moment of truth is when, after you've been kicked out of the bunkhouse and you're walking down the hall with your bag in your hand for what will be the last time and you spot the girl who defined luminescence at the end of the hall and you know that this could be the last time you ever see her and she's looking at you and you have your hand on the exit door, the door to your life after the bunkhouse, but there she is at the end of the hallway and you stop to think but your thoughts evade you—right at that moment, when all you have in your mind are the smoke trails left by thoughts and your heart is racing, that's the moment of truth.

MUD

There's black, white, and gray; so with dirt, water, and mud. It's a constant debate what's water and what's mud and what constitutes a swamp versus how much flow is needed to make a river—land and water are constantly mixing. Mud settles, is kicked up, gets dried out or made into a soup. After big storms the rivers get muddy. Some rivers look muddy even when there hasn't been a storm. Mud can be shaped, molded into a ball and thrown, applied like paint, mud can swallow things up like a mouth, can spit up rocks, sticks, turtles, and arrowheads. If it's watered down enough, the mud can move like a cloud. This is how it was in the river beneath the bridge where El Hondero and I once lived. You can cup that river water in your hands and the brown mud will swirl in it like a mist. So much mud in that water made it easy for things to float, or at least harder for things to sink all the way. Beneath the river's muddy surface, cruising invisibly along in a cloud of mud, emerging, once in a while, with just the slightest gurgle: whole trees, roots to branches, catfish bigger than a grown man, chest freezers, half-sunken boats. The muddy water made a taste in your mouth that was good at first but quickly got sour. Many legends tell of heroes who became one with mud—Hanging Frog, it is told, spent a month encased in mud, much like an arctic toad—but most people think mud is gross. By the time I hit the river on my raft of barrels I'd had more than enough run-ins with mud to understand that it would be better if I could just get along with it. Once El Hondero had disappeared, and I was left feeling entirely alone in the world, there were no reasons not to heed the muddy river's mysterious call. Sitting on the bridge alone, watching the clouds of mud slide by, listening to the river babble, watching a rusty fridge bob lazily along in the current then disappear around the green bend where the river goes behind the vines, I couldn't think of a single reason why I shouldn't go for a float myself. I thought I'd just float on the mud as far as it would take me and figure out what to do once I'd gotten there.

MAGNIFIED LIGHT

One look at the daytime sun is enough to understand the power of light. If you're out on a sunny day and you're showing skin, the sun will burn it. Hang out for just a few seconds in a beam of sunlight that's been magnified, whether through a glass lens or by the surface of the water, and you'll start to feel a burn. If the sun is high in the sky and you're floating down a river, the surface of the water all around you can be blinding. Looking at the surface of the water will be like looking into a thousand tiny mirrors all reflecting the sun at once. It will be like floating in a sea of burning light, like a sea of cold fire. Get a sheet and pull it over yourself and stay there. Pole toward the bank if there are trees overhanging the bank, and try to float in the cool green shade of canopies. Problems arise with this method. There are jetties of rock that the river people call riprap, there are huge, swirling eddies, on the riprap jetties there are fishermen who want to talk to you, some of whom are drunk, some of whom will ask to float with you, some of whom are Daddies and will actually try. Keep your river-pole handy as you float close to the bank, and stay alert. There are huge pipes belching runoff into the river, and low-hanging, snake-draped limbs that will knock you into the water. Magnified light from a bulb can create photographs (see ENLARGER) by burning shadows onto sensitive paper, and sunlight can then bleach that photograph back toward white, especially if it's magnified sunlight coming off a muddy river, especially if you've taped the photograph to the deck of your raft, and especially if the photo contains many shades of brown to begin with. The photograph of Jim 'River' Swift on his boat, the one taken by Howard Tyce (see LIBRARY), began to bleach out within a few very bright, long days on the river.

MOUTHS OF FISH
If you're floating along near the riverbank, or if you're standing by certain ponds, and the wind has pulled fluff from the buds of nearby cottonwood trees and scattered

the fluff across the surface of the water, you're going to encounter the mouths of fish. Cottonwood, a tree common along big, muddy rivers, gets its name from the balls of cotton that grow on its branches in spring. When the wind blows, thin clouds of weightless cotton float in the air, eventually coming to rest in other trees, on gravel roads, or on the water. When the cotton hits the water, the grass carp will come for it. The grass carp, the big fish that deserve the name cottonmouth as much as the white-mouthed snake, come up for the fluff and suck it down into their watery throats by opening their huge carp lips and slapping them shut. The sound of many carp mouths is a PHUP, PHUP, PHUP, and if you look you can see the cotton go under and a splash come up from where the carp mouth just was.

NEBULOUS PLANS

When someone says that such and such a plan is a nebulous one, that basically means that the person doesn't have specific expectations for how the plan is going to pan out. The word NEBULOUS comes from NEBULA, which is the name for a mysterious cluster of stars in deep space (see JOURNEY INTO DEEP SPACE). Astronomers have seen several nebulae so far, and they've all looked like hazy pictures of crabs, seahorses, and other undersea creatures spelled out in the light from stars and superheated gas clouds. A nebulous plan, then, is something distant and mostly amorphous, a plan with an ultimate goal that has not yet taken shape. Nebulous plans are often made by creatures in distress. The nebulous plan of a squab chased from its perch starts with an escape into the sky and most often ends with a return to the very same perch from which it departed, which is important to understand if you want to be a successful squabbist. The nebulous plan of a mortally betrayed orphan is to build a raft by lashing together 55-gallon plastic barrels, fixing a 10'x10' plywood platform over them, stealing a 30-foot aluminum pole from the disassembled scaffolding of a nearby construction site, boarding the raft with only a few of the most important things, and launching into the current. The image of my living father standing on the bridge from the photograph with his camera around his neck was a distant nebula until one day, while I was floating on my raft, I passed beneath a bridge that looked identical to the one in the picture. I passed a lot of run-down cabins, too, that could easily have belonged to Jim 'River' Swift, but I never thought to stop. I was preoccupied with floating, and with a vision of the ocean.

NEAR DEATH

Pull a shoelace too tight trying to secure a found buoy to the side of your raft and the lace could snap, whip you between the eyes, cause you to fall backward off the raft, and you could drown in the water. So you see, it doesn't matter whether or not you feel as if you're in danger of being killed as you live your daily life. Everything is a near-death experience.

NEXUS
The point where a series of things is held together—whether objects or ideas or life events seen in memory. The nexus of the raft is where the lines come together, the point where the ropes that run around the ten plastic barrels join up in the middle and form a knot the size of my palm, poorly but definitely tied, knots within knots. This was the spot I'd hold as the raft floated downriver on the huge vein of mud running off in the direction of the ocean. If it weren't for that knot, the barrels would have drifted apart and I'd have been left hanging on to just one. Thanks to that knot, I was able to float on my raft of barrels while seated on a step stool I'd found washed up on a jetty. I sat on my step stool beneath a little canopy of broken-down cardboard boxes, beside a cooler I'd filled with snacks and water and one or two books, along with my pencil and my pages. I'd also tied the cooler to the nexus, and what was within the cooler remained dry even when the muddy river splashed across the top of my raft, soaking my legs and feet, but it was

hot enough I didn't mind. In those days of floating I recall being way out in the middle of the water, both shores far enough away to where they looked static, and the water, floating along with me, appearing also to be unmoving except for the occasional ripples and bubbles that surfaced. I meditated on the nexus—that fat knot of rope that sucked up river water and slowly sweated it out, sometimes even creaking as it tightened. It can be very silent on the river. That knot was alive to me. By day it respired mud water and the sweat from my hands. At night I'd hold on to it when everything was so still and quiet that I thought I'd been stuck in a sinkhole of time. When it feels as if things are getting away from you, I've learned, it is best to tie up what you can, hope it's enough to float on, and hold on to the knot where it all comes together.

NIGHT RAT

A blind white rat that crosses the river at night and boards whatever floating object it encounters as it swims. The night rat is a well-mannered rat who keeps himself clean. The night rat does not fear you—his life of navigating big rivers by night (see NAVIGATING BIG RIVERS BY NIGHT) has given him a great deal of courage. You will know the night rat is coming when you hear his nails scraping along the plastic barrels of your raft. No one can say for sure why the night rat swims at night, why he is blind, or where he comes from, but I have seen one come in advance of a storm, the same way horses will run to the cover of cedars or spring peepers will start to sing in the daytime (see OMINOUS). The night rat is not to be feared, though his midnight appearance will come as a surprise. If you're lonely, you will come to appreciate him. Once the initial shock has passed, after his white fur has dried, you may even wish to stroke his coat, which he will not object to, provided you do it gently. He may show interest in the contents of your cooler. The night rat may even lift the lid of the cooler before your eyes, enter it, and begin to quietly nibble on one of the doughnuts you pulled from a dumpster. Sadly, the night rat has business on the banks and will never float with you for long.

NAVIGATING BIG RIVERS BY NIGHT
At the first sign of dusk—the squeaking of a bat, the disappearance of swifts beneath bridges—paddle out to the middle of the river. If you're in the middle of the river you're safer than you are on the shore as long as you keep an eye out for barges. You'll see the lights from people doing whatever they do at night on the banks of the river, and sometimes you'll even hear them, and when you do you'll be glad you're out there on the water alone.

OCEANS

Judging by its surface, the ocean looks like everything a mating pond is not, and on the surface it's true, but just below the ocean's surface things are mating in great numbers. On the surface the ocean looks open and infinite but it can't be infinite because it has a center point—a point that is farthest from land and closest to the moon. Here, in the middle of the ocean, nothing is going anywhere and everything is spinning in place, the wind, the waves, the wandering thunderclouds (see BOOMS), the stars, everything is spinning up the next hurricane. Here's a trick El Hondero taught me—a way he taught me to use the ocean as a tool even when you're very far from it: if ever you can't sleep, or you're anxious, or you're alone somewhere with no idea what you should do next, close your eyes and picture yourself floating on your back in the middle of the ocean. You're looking up and the stars are slowly spinning in the night sky—or you are the one spinning on the surface of the water. Feel the cool water below you. Taste the salt that laps up the side of your face. Then allow yourself to sink beneath the water, straight down, but don't stop looking up. Look up at the rippling surface of the sea as waves journey across it. Feel the void beneath you but don't look down—always up at the shining surface—and before you know it you'll be asleep.

ORDINARY NECESSITIES OF RIVER-GOING RAFTERS

You will need to use your pole to push off whatever rock or muddy shoal you get lodged upon. You will need to paddle away from large barges that are heading toward you on a collision course. You will need to maintain a low profile. You maintain a low profile while rafting down a river by traveling at night, in the fog, or, if the stretch of river is remote enough, simply by keeping a lookout for anyone going up or down the river who might try to ruin your plan (see DADDIES). You will need to find food. This need you will address with whatever fishing gear you have aboard. If it comes down to it, you can beach your raft and head out on foot. Edible mushrooms and the fine, potato-like tuber called Jerusalem Artichoke grow on the banks of rivers. Beyond the banks of rivers are roads, and along roads you can find places to buy or steal a snack. People say you can't drink the river water but you can, actually, drink it if it's fresh and you give it a minute to separate in a jar. Don't drink the mud at the bottom. If you need to sleep, it's best to pull several blankets over your head so that you completely shut out the outside world. It's hard to sleep if you're hearing the bubbles that come from unknown things in the deep murk below your raft. It's hard to sleep if you're scanning the bank for signs of

Daddies with flashlights who might also be yelling at you some things you don't want to hear. While it is true that shutting out the world while floating upon a river can be dangerous, telling yourself you're on a raft made so simply it's basically unsinkable will help put you at ease. The worst-case scenario is your getting sucked beneath a barge traveling upstream with a thousand tons of coal. Your raft might pop back up somewhere downstream, but you won't be on it.

OARMAN
A man who rows his boat with oars. Pirates, when coming ashore, do so in rowboats full of muscled oarmen. Pirates don't paddle and they don't pole rafts down rivers—they row. Another famous oarman is the one whose name I've forgotten, the one who paddled dead Greeks across the river Styx. Solitary oarmen rowing boats across rivers at night strike fear in the heart of a lone traveler, especially when the oarman, who paddles his boat facing away from where he's heading, is heading toward you. If the night is dead quiet and you're floating slowly downriver on a raft by yourself, there's a rolling fog on the water and a yellow full moon is coming up through the silhouettes of trees, and the oarman is coming toward you with his oil lamp burning grease, you have no choice, you must find the

courage to call out to him in a voice that is low but firm.
Say WHO GOES THERE, pick up your headstone, and
wait to see what he does. You may hear the wooden
thump of him knocking the oars, and the gentle drops
of water dripping from their ends, and he may turn to
you, removing his oil lamp, and from the light of it you
will see his face.

OMINOUS

If you say, "This doesn't look good," odds are it's because
you've seen something ominous: an event that you know,
through experience or intuition, precedes a second event
that's bad for you. When someone says, "We need to
talk," that's ominous. You hear a solitary oarman rowing
his way toward you in the dead of night when you're
alone and in a place where you've told nobody you're
going, that's ominous. When you look up at the sky on a
day in spring, let's say you're picking jelly beans from the
grass and the sky has turned black, that's ominous. If
you're someone who believes in signs, mystical visions,
curses, destinies, ghosts, myths where people do things
that no human should be able to do, then you're prone to
seeing omens—things that are ominous. When Hanging
Frog saw a coyote climb a tree he told everyone in the
village to build an extra canoe. A few months later, a big
flood came. That coyote was an omen because Hanging

Frog made it one. Sometimes, an omen will come to you in a dream and should cause you to change how you act when you're awake.

OVERBOARD, GOING

What has gone from being in a boat to being in the water has gone overboard. Maybe the saying comes from when all boats were made of wooden boards and anything thrown from boat into water must first have traveled over a board. For people on boats, unplanned trips overboard are almost always undesirable. To say GOING OVER-BOARD can also mean to do too much of something. My uncle went overboard with his gambling. El Hondero went overboard with his drinking on the day he lost those weather balloons. I may have gone overboard the time I put a snapping turtle in Ernesto's bunk. To say, "You've gone overboard with your lists, your catalogs, and your keys. A little handbook would suffice," is to say that some authority has put a limit to the amount of time a person should spend thinking about the language of his life.

OVERCOME BY EMOTION

Bottom of the ninth, two outs, bases loaded, home team down by three, full count. Little Ned steps into the box to take another pitch, gets his bat up. The hopes and dreams of twelve boys depend on him. Three watch from the bases, sweat stinging their eyes beneath plastic helmets, eight more lean their heads out of the dugout, hocking the sweet spit of chewing gum, some praying aloud, some silently, some boys muttering beneath their breath and wringing their hands. When Ned brings his bat up the other boys take a breath and hold it. The coaches, who have taught Ned to hold his bat this way, who've shown him how to run through first base and how to spot a hole in the outfield, are even more on edge than the players. The coaches are superstitious. They see omens and have many little rituals that they use to keep their composure under stress. The coaches' own boys are on this team and each coach would rather it be his own boy at that plate right now, but it is what it is and Ned's the one to swing and it's clear to the coaches that he doesn't stand a chance. Ned's late in the lineup. He swings at everything. When he runs, if he runs, he runs like he's hurting. He's at this game because the team brought him here, not the other way around. He plays in deep right when they're fielding and has on numerous occasions been caught sitting Indian-style, picking grass. He strolls toward fly balls. He gets called a lot of names, and has vowed to himself that this will be his last baseball season forever. Ned tightens his grip on the bat. The pitcher winds up. Moments of truth of this caliber come just three times in a person's life, five times if you're lucky. Ned knows he has to try this time. He needs to regain the feeling he had at the beginning of the season, back when the Cardinals hat his father gave him was clean and stiff, before the other boys stole it and ground it into the infield dirt, before the ball took a bad hop and knocked his braces out of whack and he sat down in the grass and cried, back, before all that, when he still had faith in the game. This time he needs to try if not just for the simple fact that his mother is in the stands, there beside his father, clapping and saying his name. She doesn't know how bad a player he is, and if she did she wouldn't care. The pitcher throws. The ball seems to move slowly through the crepuscular light. Past the outfield fence a boy is straddling his bike. Ned notices this boy as the pitcher releases the ball and is half looking at the ball and half looking at the lone boy past the outfield when he finds himself swinging, and this time it's a firm, natural cut he takes, a cut that starts at his back foot, and then a hit that sends a shock through the bat and into his hands, a sharp whack that lands on the ears of the runners who run, wide-eyed in amazement, as the coaches drop their jaws, as cans slip from the hands of spectators and tumble down the metal bleachers. Ned watches his ball rise and keep rising, rising past the left fielder, and the boy on his bike strains his head upward and shoots up his fist. Ned starts his trot toward first. The only thing he hears is his heart beating in his ears against the sides of his helmet, then up, like hiccups, come his hysterical giggles. If he could hear, he would hear the thirty onlookers in the bleachers cheering for him, and his father, hat cast off and jumping up and down, screaming his name as Ned rounds third, his father shaking with sobs of joy by the time Ned touches home. Ned's mom has her hand on his father's shoulder. She is blushing. This man, crying in the Little League bleachers, is what you would call OVERCOME BY EMOTION. This same kind of emotion can overcome you in the depths of night when you're alone and thinking of your best friend who you haven't seen since the fire because you're afraid that's where Patty would know to come looking for you. It can come as a dream. It can be fallacious. On the ninth night of my float down the river the oarman paddled out to me, raised his light, and I saw that it was El Hondero. I took the rope he threw to me and pulled us together. He'd come for me. He'd been planning this all along. He had something to tell me, and I tried to hear him, but I couldn't make out his words. He pointed downriver and I looked, saw the tar-like water shining in the moonlight, saw the swells of low hills silhouetted by distant lights far beyond the banks, but nothing new, everything was the same as it had been. When I looked back he was gone. No lamp, no rowboat, no oarman. If you're

overcome by emotion and you're alone, here's what you
do—don't try to do anything but this: lie down, curl up,
and let it wash over you.

ON THE ISLAND
When traveling downriver, after a night in which you
may or may not have encountered a ghost, you will want
to stop on an island. Find a sandbar, beach your raft, and
take a break from the float. Sometimes it can be hard to
find an island because islands like to disguise themselves
as riverbank. If you stay in the main channel it may seem
like the river has no islands when in fact there are islands
all around. Some are barely more than mud hills with
moats, others are full-blown lands of hills and forests,
caves and ponds, and all kinds of plants and animals. To
find an island you must paddle or pole along one of the
banks, staying clear of rock jetties and low-hanging
branches while keeping an eye on the river horizon.
Look for where the river splits. When you see the split,
that's the tip of an island. The best part about deciding
to stop on an island is that what's on it is always a surprise. You may find a deep oak forest with soft, leafy
ground and plenty of shade. You may climb up the muddy
shelf and find not a forest but a vast field of corn planted
neatly in rows and a low, green hill way out there like an
island in the corn. The hill, you'll think, is actually an

Indian mound that escaped the plow. There are some ancient cedar trees at its foot, and a fallen-down barbed-wire fence that weaves its way among and through them. From the top of the mound you can see the whole island.

ONCE-IN-A-LIFETIME THING
You probably won't have a chance to do it again. This is the only time this thing is going to happen to you. You're sitting alone on your raft in the middle of a day and a macaw comes and lands on your raft. A fluorescent bird, a thousand miles from its natural habitat, lands on your raft, looks at you, squawks, and flaps off. Then there was the time I watched a family of river otters transfixed by a cloud of pale-yellow butterflies. A once-in-a-lifetime opportunity is what El Hondero said the mica hunt in Ohio was, and of course he was lying, because in the end I didn't even get the one single chance. If you only have one chance to do it, at least think hard about whether or not you should. Another once-in-a-lifetime experience was the time I pulled up on the bank of the river just downstream from a huge factory. The factory was complete with skyscraping smokestacks with bright flashing lights on their tips so that airplanes wouldn't hit them in the night. When I arrived it was twilight, just beyond the crepuscular. I needed a break. I was tired, bored, didn't think much about the risks, and figured the factory was as

good a place to stop as any. People don't like to hang around near smokestacks, toxic runoff, and heavy-duty electrical equipment, and so there was not much chance I'd get caught. Chances of running into somebody right there on the bank where I'd docked, just upstream of a big culvert puking greenish water into the river? Slim to none. Which is why I froze, stunned, when I came upon a little campfire where two fat ladies from Texas were grilling chicken thighs on spears. There was the huge factory looming over us, its high metal walkways and machine sounds deafening, belching smoke that smelled of rotten eggs, and then there was the smell of grilling chicken and the two big women from Texas who were having a little cookout. They invited me over and told me they were on a road trip and asked if I was looking for a good time. They grilled me some chicken and I ate it by the fire, thanked them, said I had to pee, and slipped off in my raft. I could see their shadows projected by the light of their campfire on one of the big metal walls of the factory. They were enormous.

OPENING NEGOTIATIONS WITH A DADDY WHEN HE FINDS YOU WASHED ASHORE AND PARTIALLY DROWNED BECAUSE YOUR RAFT GOT SUCKED UNDER A BARGE WHILE YOU WERE SLEEPING

This is an impossibility. Best you can do is cry like the child you are and prepare to be hauled off to a middle-of-nowhere jailhouse.

OPERATIC FALSETTO
A high-pitched, ear-piercing singing voice that is shouted with great intensity and emotion, traditionally from the stage, traditionally during an opera, but not always. You may come into contact with an operatic falsetto in other situations, and these situations can be terrifying. The worst part is that you never know if somebody is capable of the operatic falsetto just by looking at them. If the operatic falsetto belonged exclusively to very short men with very large chests, for example, you could be on your guard around these men. There is almost no way of being prepared for the moment when a man cuts loose with his operatic falsetto. The one way you can tell that your company possesses an operatic falsetto and intends to use it is the following: when the radio starts playing opera he turns it up as high as it will go, closes his eyes, and begins to sway in his seat. If you see this, prepare yourself for the falsetto. If he then lifts a finger in the air and begins conducting, get the hell out of there as fast as you can. If you're confined to the back seat of a police cruiser and he's the sheriff in the front seat driving you God-knows-where through the

night, and if he stops his car to turn up the opera and unleash his falsetto, you will very badly want to plug your ears but you must not. Whatever you do don't plug your ears because it's most important of all, when dealing with Daddies in the wilderness, that you not offend them. Bad things have happened to orphans who have. Just look at the missing-person fliers on the corkboard outside your local supermarket. Odds are that some of those missing orphans offended a certain operatic falsettic sheriff who once picked them up where they'd washed up on the banks of a river.

OCCUPANTS OF HOLDING AREAS IN RURAL JAILS

If you are caught by an authority figure who was called by a couple of catfishermen who found you hacking up river water on the banks after your raft got sucked beneath a coal barge, he will put you in his cop car and take you wherever he wants. If you've got no identification or money or worthwhile possessions on you and look more pathetic than threatening, he will take you to a "holding area" while he tries to figure out what to do with you. In the holding area is a TV in a cage high up on the wall, three stained couches, two La-Z-Boy chairs that are bolted to the ground, a pink plastic card table with four plastic chairs, a deck with forty-nine cards, some reference handouts for drug addicts and some for people who want to be religious, a toilet with no stall around it, and a collection of Hardy Boys mysteries in paperback. You will not be alone in the holding area. The holding area will contain neighbors who, at first, are not happy to see you. Occupants of holding cells will vary from jail to jail, and they will represent the poorest people in that jail's general area. For instance, if you're taken to a jail in what turns out to be rural Louisiana, your neighbors will be a young diesel mechanic named Big-T who talks too fast and whose accent is too thick for you to understand, and a quiet, pudgy guy with a ponytail who reeks of alcohol and has skin like paste, whose balding head, above the ponytail, flakes like wax, and who has an enormous tattoo of a Betta Fish on his neck. The neighbors of your holding area will be glued to the television, which, in its iron cage, is broadcasting reruns of the TV show COPS. If you interrupt him as he's trying to watch COPS to ask about the Betta Fish on his neck, an occupant of a holding area in a rural jail cell will say, in a way that actually sounds friendly, that he'll tell you what the Betta Fish means if you let him give you a black eye, and then you'll have to decide if it's worth it.

PORKING

If when you come home early you walk in on your fiancée and a man you don't know having sex in the kitchen of your house, you've found them porking. If you come home and find that a stranger is porking your fiancée in the kitchen of your house you'll become angry (see MORTAL BETRAYAL) and lose control of yourself (see OVERBOARD, GOING). Most often the porker will run off into the woods after you hit him with a chair and tell him to get out, and, an hour after, you and your fiancée will be trying to get back on good terms again. If the porker is a lawyer, on the other hand, and you hit him with a chair and he runs off into the woods, just as you and your fiancée are making up the sheriff will show up and take you to the holding area. Once you're there, you'll want to make yourself feel better about the whole episode by telling the strangers who are in the holding area with you all about what happened.

PEACEFUL NEUTRALITY

If you're new to a holding area, chances are you won't be receiving a warm welcome from your new neighbors. Over time, if you're polite (see GOOD MANNERS, THE IMPORTANCE OF), your neighbors may seem to get used to your presence. Once this period of adjustment has passed, you'll be asked to take sides. The occasion of your choosing a side will involve a conflict among your neighbors in the holding cell. If, say, one guy wants to switch the channel because he's been watching nothing but COPS reruns for days and, say, the other guy would rather watch COPS than the only other available channel, which is showing vintage LOONEY TUNES, and, he says, "Elmer Fudd ain't funny," you may be asked to cast a tic-breaking vote. It is important that you not voice an opinion, even if you have one, since voicing an opinion will make a friend of one of the men but a mortal enemy of the other and, in this case, subscribing to one team and not to the other will officially make you part of whatever game or competition or conflict that may arise in the rest of your time in the holding cell.

PISSING YOUR PANTS

This is a phrase that is used to describe a state of extreme fear. Let's say you're sharing a holding area with two men who are much larger than you, whose speech you find hard to understand, and whose violent outbursts come mostly at random. These are men you've just met, whom you know nothing about, who've committed any number of strange, elaborate, twisted crimes in recent nights before eventually winding up locked in here, with you. They wind up here so often that it's like a living room for them. They know how to fix the broken television so it works and they know which of the tables isn't bolted to the floor of the holding area and they've even hidden cigarettes in a BIBLE with a hollow place in it that's one of the only books on the little shelf. Let's say that the appearance of Elmer Fudd on a television screen in that holding area causes a man with waxy skin and a tattoo on his neck to beat another man in the holding area with a plastic card table. Let's say you abandon peaceful neutrality to intervene in the conflict and are subsequently threatened with the plastic table. You might, at that point, be pissing your pants.

PATROLS AT NIGHT

The job of someone who patrols at night is to keep an eye on a place between dusk and dawn, when people should be sleeping and nothing should require attention but when most evil things usually happen. The night patrol checks to see that all the locks are still locked, that the drips dripping from the air conditioners haven't over-filled the cups that catch them. He checks to see that the vending machine is stocked, that all the pencils in a cup on the lieutenant's desk are sharp. At any moment in the night, he might be called out to a blood-covered living room in a nearby trailer and asked to make photographs of dead people. He walks past the holding room and looks inside. He's supposed to do this every couple of hours. The night patrol must be cool-headed but firm and, in principle, he must uphold the rules of the institution he patrols. Between patrols, he can be found reading a book or listening to the radio at a desk down the hall from the holding area. If he's like the night patrol at the jail whose holding area you've occupied for thirty-six hours after having washed ashore on the banks of a river, who finds you huddled in a corner of the holding area during the course of his patrol, he'll take you from that holding area, give you a soda and a candy bar from the vending machine, and ask you to tell him your story. If you tell your story right he'll make some notes on some papers, lean in to show he's listening, and once you're done telling your story he'll tell you his. It'll be late and you'll be exhausted and it might be boring to hear him talk about his job but you must try to stay awake. It's bad manners to fall asleep when people are talking to you. When he's done talking he'll let you take a shower in the employee locker room and then, just before dawn, he'll give you a ride to the nearest bus station where he'll instruct you to wait for the afternoon bus going north. In the idling car he'll hand you a little garbage bag in which you'll find another garbage bag—the one you thought you'd lost in the shipwreck—and inside that bag you'll find your papers, the photograph of your dad, and the arrowhead you picked up on the island upriver. He'll apologize on behalf of the operatic falsettic sheriff and he'll thank you for listening to him talk for a while, and then he'll leave. You often find lonely people in the most unlikely places.

PODUNK TOWN

On the surface, in the eyes of a visitor, a Podunk Town has no distinguishing characteristics. In reality, every Podunk Town has its own set of laws, rules, guidelines, and specialized terms. Nearly all Podunk Towns have a dollar store, a McDonald's, a car repair shop, a religious antique store, a bus stop, and a gas station. In most Podunk Towns, one or two people will be sitting up against a dumpster in the gas-station parking lot drinking beer from forty-ounce glass bottles. The sidewalks of a Podunk Town are mostly empty. Cars can be seen idling in the dollar-store parking lot and in lines at the drive-thru. Killing time in a Podunk Town can be a chore if all you have is a few dollars and a bus ticket. The first thing to do is check the dollar-store dumpster for stationery supplies and expired snacks. Avoid the locals as you do this. If the Podunk Town you're in is the home of the sheriff who has recently arrested you on unfounded charges of trespassing, theft, and conspiracy to burglarize, be especially careful not to attract attention to yourself. Scan the ground for dropped money or bills that have been sucked by wind from cars idling at the drive-thru. The bushes around drive-thrus often contain bills in their thorns. If, when you check the bushes, you find ten bucks, and you're bored and depressed because your raft was sucked beneath a barge, it's a good idea to approach the two men by the dumpster with your money and have them buy you one of those big beers. Maybe one of them is in Real Estate. You must hope that neither of these men is a Daddy.

Be careful that they give you enough change when they give you your bottle of beer, but don't count it in front of them because it's rude to act like they're not trustworthy, and then tip them a dollar for their efforts. When they ask you where you're going, say Paducah, unless of course you are actually going to Paducah, in which case tell them Poughkeepsie. If you're lucky, whatever Podunk Town you get stuck in will also be near a river and a bridge or at least a culvert where you can go to get out of the sun for a while.

PHILOSOPHY OF NIHILISM
Nihilism is the idea that nothing you do matters, that no belief you have will improve your life or the lives of those around you. Nihilism is a perfectly logical response to an overwhelming and confusing world. Butch, the waxy man with a tattoo on his neck in the holding area, was a good example of a nihilist. The only time he seemed to care about anything was when Elmer Fudd came on TV, and that was because something was seriously wrong inside of his head. In fact, the back of Butch's skull had a square scar, which had to be from where a doctor took part of his brain out. Butch was a guy who didn't seem to want to be in his own brain any longer than he had to.

The night patrol, unlike Butch, believed there was a right and a wrong way to live in this world, and he believed it was wrong to keep me locked up in the holding area. I hadn't hurt anyone, and still there I was about to be beaten with a plastic card table by a man I'd never met before. If you're saved from a bad situation by someone who is not a nihilist, like the night patrol, that doesn't mean you won't do something nihilist yourself. Let's say you're alone at a bus stop in a Podunk Town along a river in the middle of nowhere. Let's say you're feeling leery of strangers, and your stomach is growling, and that it's an hour before your bus leaves. Let's say your sole concern becomes getting some food in your stomach, and let's say there's a man selling hot dogs off hot metal rollers in the corner of the bus station. If you believe it is wrong to steal because stealing hurts other people, you will not steal hot dogs from the hot-dog man. On the other hand, if you see the universe as a chaotic soup in which you're slowly being boiled, and you've been shown, time and time again, that no matter how you act, things will come along and change your life in ways over which you have no control, you will.

PURPOSE
Related to EXPECTATION, purpose is a feeling that one thing is related to another by being the cause of it, the

reason for the second thing. We need an example: THE PURPOSE OF THE BAT IS TO HIT THE BASEBALL. See how we expect there to be nothing that comes along before a baseball that the bat needs to hit? Still, almost no one would argue with the statement THE PURPOSE OF THE BAT IS TO HIT THE BASEBALL. Human beings spend a lot of time and energy trying to understand the behavior of one another. A boy convinces himself he has understood why someone is doing something by coming up with a reason why that person is doing that thing—a purpose for that person's action. Why is a man climbing that tree with a bugle in his belt? Because he wants to play the bugle from a tree limb. There's his purpose.

QUANTIFIABLE
Numbers are comforting. Anything you can put a number to is a quantifiable thing. A river is not a quantifiable thing, but the gallons of water flowing through a culvert each minute can be counted, made into a numerical quantity, which means QUANTIFIED. You don't actually have to count something for that thing to be quantifiable, you just have to know that you could count it if you wanted to. Whether or not animals quantify anything is a mystery, but there must come a point in time when a squirrel stops squirreling his nuts—a point

in time where he judges he's got enough. Does that mean he has quantified his nuts, or could he just have looked at his nut pile and thought "Big enough." The question of whether or not animals quantify things is probably impossible to answer. An eagle would, you would hope, notice a chick is missing if when she left the nest there were three chicks and when she returned there were two. You would hope. You assume the gypsy knows what he's doing when he looks at your car, pockmarked all over by hail, and says "I see around seventy-seven dents," which is quantifying your problem. Numbers are supposed to establish certainty, but they don't always. The photograph by Howard Tyce, torn from the library book by El Hondero and stolen from me by the river, was published long before I launched my little raft, but not long after he'd left me with my uncle. The photograph was taken some quantity of time before it came out in the book, let's say a few months, and round up, so let's say ten years before I got on the river the photograph was taken, and so ten years plus three weeks, give or take a few days, before I arrived, unknowingly, in the place where the photograph was taken. Do these quantities help? How could they? I don't have an idea how many hot dogs I have stolen over the years. Maybe knowing the total number would be comforting. If you're trying to kill time, let's say you're feeling lonely and confused, try quantifying something. Take for instance the squabs perched on the power line outside the dollar store. There are exactly twelve of them. When a new squab flies up and perches, one of the old squabs drops from the line and flies away, and so it's still twelve squabs. When three squabs fly up and land on the line together, no original squabs leave, though one seems like he's about to and then doesn't, and so the number of squabs is now fifteen. The population of squabs on the power line outside the dollar store somehow becomes important once you've quantified it. Nobody can tell you why the squabs have become important—it's probably just that numbers are comforting the same way lists and definitions are comforting, the same way a campfire (see CAMPFIRE) in the night is comforting. The number of times I've quantified things like squabs on a line in order to feel the comfort of a number? Countless times. The method works for a moment, but then everything that's not quantifiable surges like water through a culvert after a storm.

QUESTIONABLE

If something is questionable it means it might not work, or that you don't believe it's true. The purpose of the word QUESTIONABLE is itself questionable. "Those monkey bars are questionable," people said, for instance, about the old wooden monkey bars in the overgrown yard behind the Wilson Carmichael Bunkhouse. When a fat boy tried the monkey bars, he quantified the maximum weight the rotting rungs could hold to be the weight of one fat boy. He made it down the bars with no trouble. When a skinny boy went next, the fifth rung broke in his left hand as he swung toward the sixth rung, his right arm outstretched, and so the quantity had changed. The maximum load of the remaining monkey bars became questionable again. Everything can be questionable. A nihilist no longer questions anything because no answer has ever really helped him. To a nihilist, the world is soup, and counting squabs is useful only if he's wondering about dinner. I remember there were nights in my uncle's mansion when I questioned if my body would work without the help of my mind. I worried that I'd forget to breathe and die in the night, and I wouldn't fall asleep until he sat there with me and held my hand in the dark.

REVELATION

A moment when something becomes clear to you all at once. Revelations come without warning and at random, and sometimes they come at just the right time. You can spend days and days or even years thinking through a mystery and then have the solution come to you when you're sitting on a porch listening to a baseball game on a little radio. You can be lost, your future unclear, without a single thing you can think of that you have to do or even that you should do, and then a revelation will hit you and your mind will instantly be made up. You can be standing at a bus stop when you notice, from the corner of your eye, something that causes a revelation. You see something you recognize but you don't know why, and then all of a sudden you do. When I was waiting for the bus in the Podunk Town by the river, I noticed from the corner of my eye an old man walking with a cane along an overgrown footpath that led steeply down to the banks. Vines hung over the path. The sight of this old man walking alone toward the river, parting the vines—I'd seen it before (see MYSTICAL VISION). Then he looked at me. He looked for a moment longer than you'd look at a random stranger, as if he recognized me, and then I recognized HIM, and then came the revelation that I was here in this Podunk Town for a very specific reason and that reason was this old man, named Jim 'River' Swift, who hadn't aged much in the years since my father had taken his photograph. I got up, walked away from the bus stop and down the path after him, back to that river which just a few days earlier had tried to drown me.

RUM RUNNER

An alcoholic drink named after famous booze-hustling pirates, a drink invented by people who lived on an island somewhere in the tropics—perhaps Dominica. Over time, the rum runner gained favor among people not living on that island, and the original recipe changed. Originally, the rum runner was meant to be drunk from cups made of coconuts. The recipe called for rum, fresh juices, and herbs. Over time, the rum runner made its way inland, changing as the recipe was passed from drinker to drinker, eventually penetrating to the heart of the largest continents. Ask an old guy who lives in a shack on the banks of a muddy river in Middle America to make a rum runner and what he'll make will come in a blue plastic cup with a nibbled rim. In the cup he'll put pale, cloudy ice, several long glugs of Seaman's Best white rum, and a splash of Sunny Delight.

RUMINATIONS OF THE ELDERLY

If you happen upon a lonely old man living by himself in a houseboat on a river and you stop by to talk to him, let's say you stop by on the pretext of asking for some advice about fishing in the area but then instead ask him if he remembers someone you think he met many years earlier, expect this elder to ruminate. If you've been to a nursing home, you've heard the elderly ruminating. If you have to use a cane to get from place to place and require frequent rests, you will find that your days become filled with less doing and more ruminating. When you meet an elder and ask him a question, he will begin to talk, and his answer to a simple question will end up being an answer to a lot of questions you didn't ask. An old man with the need to ruminate will pop like a champagne bottle when you ask him a question and the stories will come out like the foam. It will be impossible to get the cork back in the bottle and anyway it would be rude to try because elders left by themselves most of the time can't entertain themselves like they once did and need to take that lost liveliness and apply it to ruminating. Let the old man by the river talk and sit still, nod, and listen. Answer his questions, even if they're ones with obvious answers, answer them in a way that keeps the old man ruminating. If you want a specific answer to a specific question, and you need to ask an elder in order to get your information, you must be prepared to listen for a long time. He will mention names of people as if you know who he's talking about. He will make guesses about what kind of person you are from the way you look, and no matter how wrong he is you must not correct him. Let's say he's an old hermit who you've followed down a path to the shack by the river where he lives. You think you recognize the man from a photograph taken by your father, and you figure it's worth a shot to ask this old man if he remembers anything. Your hopes should not be high, since elders who live in shacks on the banks of rivers often look alike, and there are a dozen big, muddy rivers like the one in the photograph, and anyway there's almost zero chance that this elder would remember having his picture taken years ago by a passing photographer. But still, whether you like it or not, there's something that fills you with hope. Upriver from the houseboat there's a suspension bridge that looks like the one in the picture taken by Howard Tyce. Ask the elder if his name is Jim.

SARDINES A LA KETCHUP
A sardine is a tiny fish that tastes like salt. A and LA are French words that mean IN and THE. Ketchup speaks for itself. It's unclear how this dish earned its French name, since it didn't originate anywhere near the country of France. SARDINES A LA KETCHUP is a dish prized by old men who live alone on the banks of rivers. If you never have a chance to try SARDINES A LA KETCHUP, you're not missing out. If you had to choose between it and Salisbury Steak, you'd be wise to go with the steak. If somebody offers you SARDINES A LA KETCHUP, and you're very, very hungry, it would still be best to ask for just the sardines or just the ketchup.

SAYNKER

This is the word, among river folk, for anything that sinks to the bottom of a body of water when you throw it in and that's heavy enough to drag fish hook, bait, and line down to the bottom of the river with it. A saynker's got to be heavy if the river current is swift. If river folk say "Use it as a saynker," they intend for you to tie it, whatever it is, car part, brick, or glass eye, to a fishing line and throw it in the water. While it may be hard to believe about the glass eye, it's a fact that a man named Biggs, an acquaintance of Jim 'River' Swift and fellow fan of the rum runner, uses his lucky eye as a saynker when fishing for catfish, and it works. There's a little hole through his glass eye so all he has to do is pop the eye out with his thumb, thread it on the line, and toss it overboard.

SEEING UNDERWATER

Seeing underwater depends on the water and on the eye that's doing the seeing. If it hasn't rained in a while and the water you want to see in hasn't flowed through any place with banks too muddy and if your eyes aren't too sensitive you can put your head under the water, open your eyes, and see things. Some of the little creeks that come trickling into big rivers are clear enough to see in. Sometimes these little creeks will be springs, and you'll know this because they're cold and crystal clear like a fish tank and you can keep your eyes open for a long time in the pure water. If it's a pond you want to see in, say it's a small pond dug out of what was once the forest floor and now is filled in with rain, ringed with cattails and patrolled by carp, don't expect to see anything underwater. Even if you have a good pair of goggles and a flashlight, all you'll be able to see is swirling clouds of brown and whatever comes within a foot of your face.

SLEEPING ON THE FLOOR

While generally this is something people try to avoid doing without the help of some kind of mattress, there are certain instances where furniture is present and there is no mattress, there is not even paper to make a paper mattress, and yet sleeping on the floor seems like the best option. Perhaps there are beetles with large mandibles crawling around on the couch, using the insides of the cushions as a place to lay eggs. And perhaps when you go to sit on the La-Z-Boy you find that the seat is oddly wet and funny smelling. If you decide to sleep on the floor, wrap yourself up in a sheet like you'd wrap a burrito or an egg roll, including, especially, your head. You'll want to sleep with your head covered so nothing can get inside your mouth. Nothing is worse than waking up to the touch of the night rat's long-nailed paw on your lip. If you can't find a sheet to wrap yourself in, a tacky truck-stop wolf-and-Indian tapestry taken down from a wall will do the trick. If you see, on the wall beside the tapestry, in a plastic frame, the photograph by Howard Tyce, you might find it hard to sleep, even with the truck-stop tapestry protecting you.

SKINNY-DIP

The act of swimming in the nude. Skinny-dipping is the most natural way to swim. It's the way we were meant to be in the water. A good dip in the nude, at dawn, in a broad, softly gurgling river, in the summer, is maybe the healthiest and most refreshing thing a person can do. I learned this from Jim, who said that skinny-dipping every day at dawn was the secret to immortality. This is because every time you do it you're letting your soul experience what it felt when it was born—you came out in the nude, the womb had water in it like a river, and the light of the room into which you were born was like the sunrise. Coming out of the river and feeling the sun's first rays bite through the chill of dawn air allows the mind to open, to do its best hard thinking, to solve problems that have been bothering it, and to recall things it had forgotten (see KERNELS OF THE PAST).

SPEAKING CLEARLY

People are hard to understand on many levels, but especially when they're talking. You can get a lot of information from people just by watching them for a little while. It's when they speak that the problems of communication come out.

SKIPPING ROCKS

Stones that are flat, smooth, somewhat roundish, and no larger than your hand can be whipped sidearm in such a way that they bounce across the surface of a body of water. Depending on the force of the throw, the angle of the release, the stance assumed by the person skipping, and the wind, a skipping rock can travel as far as fifty yards, touching the water up to seven or eight times before finally sinking or landing on the opposite bank. Skipping takes a lot of practice for most people. Most people will only get a rock to skip every once in a while, and even then they'll only be able to get it to go two or three skips. I can't tell you how many people I've seen throw down their rocks and stomp away from the riverbank. What most people need is a good teacher, a decent pond to start out on, and patience. Others seem to have been born with the ability to skip a rock. Some of those people go on to enter rock-skipping competitions and can get very serious about it. For some people, rock skipping is a form of therapy. Jim, for example, swore that he'd skipped at least seven rocks a day since he was five years old. In the morning following the night when I slept on the floor of his shack, after we'd taken a skinny dip, he and I skipped rocks across the river. "You're a damn fine skipper," he said, as a blueish stone I'd thrown took its last flutter of skips and sank halfway across. Then he said: "Your old man was good at it, too. We skipped rocks every time he came down here. Seemed about the first thing he'd do every time he showed up was go down to the beach, find some rocks, and skip them—not say nothing to nobody until he'd finished. That was always how it was. We never did know when he'd come and when he'd go, but if you saw that little car coming down the river road you could count on him to walk down here and start skipping," and that was the first time I was introduced to the idea that a gift for rock skipping could be passed on from parent to child.

At that moment, by the river with River Jim, you realize that by skipping things across a surface you're defining not just the tension of that surface but also the weight of the thing that's skipping. You realize your ability to define the story of what happened, and you feel the courage to tell a story in your own words—the proper way—so it can't be rewritten. It's about writing your life on the face of the world in such a way that you and the world, both, are made real.

SANITY

This is a term used to describe the ability of a person to

behave normally. Behavior that you see as normal you call SANE behavior. Sanity is at best a very loose idea since you can do something in one situation and have it be seen as sane while you can do that same thing in another situation and have it be seen as a sign that you've lost your sanity. Throw a rock into a pond so that it skips, that's a perfectly sane thing to do. If you were to try to skip, say, ancient mica artifacts, you might be seen as having lost your sanity. If you and all your family and friends got together and spent fifty years building a mound of earth in your backyard and you didn't bury anybody underneath it and you didn't put some kind of a fort on top of it, but instead you just went up to the top of the mound, put your hands on your hips, and said, at the top of your lungs, "It's done," you might be called insane. We've all done something that would make it look, if someone had seen us do it, like we were out of our mind, or insane. Probably the most famous example of a loss of sanity is suicide, but in some situations you might be acting logically because, as best as you can tell, the reasons to die generally outweigh the reasons to live. The reasons for living become questionable, and then eventually you quantify them as zero.

STEALING WOMEN

It's not like stealing money, which is a concept everybody is familiar with. Stealing a woman means you got her to love you, when before, she had loved somebody else. This is understood as a form of mortal betrayal. No matter who you betrayed, it must not feel good to have people think you're a stolen woman as opposed to just thinking of you as a woman who changed her mind. River Jim said he thought my dad came down to the river to get away after somebody stole his woman, and that a lot of people down by the river had had their woman stolen at one time or another, including him. He told me all about a woman named Janet, whom he used to love but who sold her soul to alcohol and then got stolen by a man who worked as the director of the chamber of commerce in Paducah. I asked if he'd found them porking, and he said that in fact he had. Then I told him that the particular stolen woman he'd referred to earlier was my mother, and that I'd never heard of her being owned by anybody, but now she was dead and so it didn't matter—the earth owned her, or whatever—and a funny look came over Jim's face and he apologized once or twice before going in to make another rum runner.

When he came out, he had the drink in one hand and a cardboard shoebox in the other. He handed it to me, and the box was heavy.

"I hadn't stole this," Jim said. "Just been holding it. I guess it's yours."

I opened the box and found a camera inside.

SWIMMING BIG RIVERS

If you're by a river and it's hot out and you want to cool off and the water is moving slowly along, gurgling or rushing in the inviting way some rivers do, you might feel the need to get in that water. This can be a good or a bad idea. It's a good idea to swim the big river if it's a clear night and the full moon is out so you can see the water is moving calmly and without much debris. Swim out, lie on your back, float for a while, look at the sky, and then pick a safe spot to climb back ashore. It's a good idea to swim the big river if you're floating on a raft in the middle of the big river, it's hot out and the reflection of the sun on the muddy water is blinding, and there's a little rope attached to your raft that you can tie around your waist while you float along at the same, natural pace as the river and the raft. But it's a bad idea to swim a big river if the water is full of huge logs that have been swept into the water by a flood somewhere upstream. It's a bad idea to swim a big river if the water is so high that it has engulfed a living forest. It's a bad idea to dive into the big river if it's thunderstorming. Diving into a big river at night, when it's thunderstorming and the river is filled with ancient trees that have been torn, roots and all, from the shore somewhere upstream, is what river folk call insane. If you're hanging out near a river taking photographs of the people living on the river's banks, and you've been there for a few days so the local people have gotten to know you and you them, and you know about the dangers of swimming big rivers, and you know about thunderstorms and you know about saynkers, and you know about floating and you know about rum runners, you have shown that you can do what it takes to live life as an adult. If this is you, and yet you jump into a flooding river at night when it's thunderstorming out, and you've left your possessions boxed neatly in the trunk of your car, and people see you do this—they see you get in the river while rain is pouring and lightning flashing and they see you paddle out into a current so violent it's got huge trees spinning circles in its eddies—and they don't see you come back to shore, they know you have abandoned your sanity. You've abandoned your life.

SHAMAN

A person who can travel to the spirit world and come back from there with information. A shaman can also be a healer (see MEDICINE PEOPLE) and will have a good collection of powerful trinkets. A shaman only works if you believe in him. If you believe in him, the things he tells you about the spirit world might come to help you. While a true shaman can look like anybody, those painters who make the art that's sold at truck stops have a very specific idea of what a shaman should look like. Take, for instance, the faded tapestry that Jim had hung on the inside wall of his shack. In the tapestry a shaman stands on a mountaintop at night. A big storm cloud with a face in it looms over him. A full moon is shining through the thunderhead. The shaman is a mostly nude, muscular Indian, who has deer antlers on his head. He's holding a long staff with powerful stones in its gnarled tip. He wears a serious, concerned expression on his face, and his eyes look up at the thunderhead. He wears a fox-pelt loincloth, and his two pet wolves, one on either side of him, are howling. You'll know you're looking at a work of truck-stop shaman art if you're seeing wolves howling in close proximity to people. The sad truth about shamans is that you can believe in a shaman one day and then not believe in him the next, and in that way you can make all his power disappear. If I'd seen a shaman poster on a wall in my parents' bus or my uncle's mansion, for example, I'd have been able to feel the shaman's power—I'd have been able to control the thunder and lightning, change jelly beans into horses, float through deep space on the inside of a balloon, or make wolves and coyotes do my bidding. When El Hondero told me about Hanging Frog and the shamans who made the mica hands, I knew that all I had to do to get powers like theirs was to make my own version of the mica hand, to write my own history, and then I'd be able to have some power over the world. Then I found out about how my father took photographs, summoned them like a shaman from burned and washed paper (see ENLARGER), left me with my uncle, drove down the river, took some photos there, and then, for reasons that had to do with the stealing of women, lost his sanity and went for a swim in a thunderstorm. When you hear something like that last part, the spirit world becomes cheap and tacky, and a lie.

SEASONS

Kids learn about spring, summer, fall, and winter. These are all made-up. These made-up seasons sometimes go by other made-up names. Within these four made-up seasons there are countless other made-up seasons. Somewhere in fall comes the season of making hand turkeys with construction paper and brown finger paint. In winter, once the ponds have frozen, comes ice-skating season. Summer is swimming season, though you can swim in the other seasons if you don't mind being cold. Fall: pumpkin season. Pumpkins grow all summer, too, but their official season is the one when they get ripped off the plant. Anything can be a season if you say it is. Rafting season starts in late summer and runs through early fall, past the tail-end of swimming season. If ever I raft in other seasons, rafting season will expand to

include that other season. After rafting season comes
smell-of-rotten-leaves season. Sweater season stretches
through fall, winter, and some of spring, depending on
where you are. It was summer when my uncle got in the
back seat of a police car, and in that season he was only
wearing a t-shirt. When autumn came, that's when I
started picturing him shivering in his concrete cell. By
then I'd given up thinking that strong daydreams were
mystical visions from some kind of a spirit realm. I even
quit believing in the one I had, on the bridge, before I got
on the raft, the vision in which I'd seen River Jim. I told
myself that all the visions I'd ever had were ones I'd
invented, and that I could imagine whatever I wanted, so
I envisioned a prison sweater on my uncle and felt a little
better with this made-up image. I envisioned the gypsies
in the Florida Keys selling coral and shells on the roadside
and painting the hulls of boats for money. I pictured El
Hondero in Ohio, where he was at the tail-end of digging
season. I saw him digging alone, in the woods, leaves falling all around him, looking for the mother lode, and saw
that he'd found not a single piece of mica, that he was
suffering trench foot, and that his teeth were ground flat
because he'd been living on acorns for weeks. I smiled and
then felt sad—emotions have very short seasons. Standing
in the yard of Jim's shack on the banks of the river I
imagined that I was my father, so many seasons ago, and

I held my hands up and made a square with my fingers, put the river in the square, and the river seemed to run faster when I did that. When I dropped my hands the river slowed back down. I heard the ice in Jim's rum runner, then I felt his hand on my shoulder, and with that the season of revelations reached its end and I was ready to leave the river.

TANGLED LINE

Every line will tangle itself if you give it a chance, and everyone has been beaten by at least one tangle. Jute rope has a will: it wants to tangle itself. Line has a mind like an animal. Wet hair, the same. To untangle a tangle, your willpower must be more than that of the line. There are piles of orange extension cord tangled in weeds outside shacks on the banks of rivers. Let them lie.

TAKEOFF

When something takes off it doesn't necessarily take anything but itself off and usually what it's taking itself off of is the ground, as in the case of a plane or a fleeing goose, but it doesn't have to, it can also take off down a road or down a river or through the woods or on a train. If you meet a sad-looking woman in a parking lot beside a car with one of its side-view mirrors broken and dangling and you ask her, "What happened?" and she says,

"He hit me and he just took off," you can be sure she's referring to another motorist rather than somebody taxiing around in an airplane, although there is a bruise on her face and so you can't be totally sure what hit her, where she was when it happened, and how it happened. If you yourself have recently left the place where you were staying for the night, let's say a place where you could no longer stand to be, you will realize that someone at that same moment might be saying, "He just took off," in reference to you. You might see this as a coincidence. What takes off must arrive somewhere other than where it came from. If the woman beside the car asks your name and where you're from and you tell her, because she has the eyes of someone nice, and then when she asks you where you're headed you say, "Anywhere, as long as it's away from that river," she might take this as an opportunity to offer you a seat in her car and the two of you might, together, take off.

TOY DOG

A miniature version of a particular dog breed. There are very few toy-dog mutts (see BREEDING DOGS) because most toy dogs can't survive for long in the wild. Chihuahuas, on the other hand, a small breed by nature yet not technically toy, are excellent survivalists and will often sire litters of mutts in wilderness dens. Toy dogs are made the size of toys by breeders who choose the runts of normal-size dogs as breeding stock, then the runts of those runts, then the runts of those runts, and so on until what would usually be a midsize dog can now, even at maturity, be kept in a red leather purse. Toy dogs are hypervigilant and almost always on edge. They can look in two directions at once, possibly as an evolved defensive mechanism, or possibly because their breeders tried to make too many changes over too few generations. If you get in a car with a stranger (see GETTING IN CARS WITH STRANGERS) and a Pekingese toy dog in a red leather purse occupies the passenger seat, where the driver has indicated that you're meant to sit, it's good manners to take the bagged Pekingese on your lap and to stroke its quivering, ratlike head as the car takes off. Toy dogs are very sensitive and must be treated with tenderness (see TENDERNESS), especially if the owner of the toy dog is giving you a free ride somewhere.

TALKER
Someone who starts talking and doesn't stop for a long time, frequently moving from one subject to another and talking about that second subject for a while before continuing to yet another subject without once taking a break. There are several subvarieties of talkers, some

you'll be able to understand and others you won't, kind
of like radio stations. Talkers will go on talking whether
or not you're talking back or even listening. Some talkers
are people who have recently spent a lot of time alone, or
have something very important to say and once they have
they'll be quiet. These are the quick-tale talkers.
Compared to some other people I've met, the night patrol
officer was one. Compared to some people, he was easy
to listen to. River Jim, on the other hand, was not so easy
to listen to. His talk was typical of the ruminations of the
elderly. It traveled across time, went from place to place,
name to name, and thing to thing. In a five-minute span
I heard him talk about President Nixon and how to trap
beavers and the Kansas City Royals and why the bacon
at the dollar store was going up in price. A talker would
be easy to understand if you had some reference guide
you could use to decipher him, but usually you don't. You
knew River Jim expected you to know something about
what he was talking about when he leaned in, gave your
ribs a little jab with his elbow, and laughed in such a way
that it would be bad manners not to laugh along with
him. Sabi Juarez, whose car got hit in the parking lot just
before I got in it, was an easy-listening-type talker. She
had a sharp Mexican accent. The consonants were all
sticky and bouncing around her teeth, and she sometimes dragged a vowel way, way out. Sabi was also fun to

watch as she talked. Her hands, most of the time, were somewhere in the air near her head, even when she was driving. Her hair was charcoal black and very curly, just like El Hondero's. Her fingernails were a bright red with no chips taken out of the paint, and they went in and out of her hair, which shook and swept like a flock of birds or something as she drove me along and fluffed it and talked. Sabi told stories about her ex-husband and his obsession with conspiracy theories, his terrible habit of sleepwalking, and her terrible luck with cars. She talked about her telemarketing job and the people she worked with, how they stole things from her cubicle, how she deflated their tires as revenge, how she'd had terrible bad luck with her first car, a Chrysler LeBaron, how she'd vowed, at age sixteen, never to spend over three hundred dollars on either a car or repairs for a car because any time you spent money on a used car you were gambling and she hated gambling, how she hasn't to this day gambled on anything but scratch-off tickets and on cars because gambling on cars and scratchers isn't real gambling, technically, and though she'd had mostly bad luck with her cars, she'd had some good luck, too, like the one Jeep that ran for ten years. The car we were in, a station wagon with hail damage and a cracked windshield, ran fine but now it had a side-view mirror missing because "some gringo in a silver pickup ran right into it and just took off" shortly before I walked past Sabi in the parking lot. She asked me again if I'd seen him, the guy who did it, and I said, again, that I hadn't, but I'd heard it, because I was close by but focused on counting the number of squabs on the power line. There were white squabs, albinos, a good-sized population, there were black-and-brown squabs, too, and I was pretty sure there was at least one blue squab up there on the line. I asked if she'd ever eaten squab, and she said no, but Chicken Teriyaki was her favorite food. She asked me questions about my life and seemed to find what I said wildly interesting. When I couldn't answer a question, she supplied an answer for me.

TRIAL DATABASE

If you break the law and you get taken off to jail, it can take a while before the court gets around to making a solid decision about how long it's going to keep you locked up before it gives you your trial. When it decides what day it wants you to go on trial, it publishes the date and time on a trial database, which you can look up online. Sabi's apartment was at the end of a cul-de-sac in a suburb where there were dozens of other two-story apartment buildings that looked just like hers all joined together side by side in front of a deep forest of sycamore and oak trees. Her computer monitor was on a desk next

to a cushion where the Chihuahua was sitting, chewing
on his stick of leather, a little bell on his collar jingling
as he chewed the mud-colored leather stick until it was
white and spitty and flat and he could eat it. Sabi showed
me how to look through the trial database online. Her
ex-husband, for instance, had a trial in a month. She
planned on going there and telling the judge to lock him
up forever, but maybe she would tell the judge to let him
go, she couldn't say for sure. It all depended on whether
or not she'd forgiven him by the time of the trial. When
we looked up my uncle's name on the internet we found
out that he was going on trial in a week.

TELENOVELA
Spanish for a TV novel, a TELENOVELA is a TV show
where people have their lives ripped apart by love. All the
major emotions play out in the telenovela: jealousy, mortal
betrayal, coincidence, homicide, Little League, mating,
expectation, boredom . . . Telenovelas come in weird,
dreamlike, glittery color. The women wear lots of makeup.
If you don't speak Spanish you won't be able to understand
what the telenovela people are saying but you can gather
what's going on from their tone of voice and by watching
what they do. Even the Chihuahua seems to understand
when something important is happening, but this is
probably because he reacts to the way Sabi is reacting to

the plot. The Chihuahua gives either a whine or a yip depending on Sabi's reaction. Telenovelas are more interesting to watch if you're watching with somebody who fills you in on some of the important words here and there because she knows Spanish and is for some reason interested in making your telenovela experience a more pleasurable one. Even if you'd be happy to just watch the melodramatic actors walk around getting emotional in the glimmering light, even if you could just sit there and let the Spanish wash over you, it's bad manners not to act riveted by the translation of a woman like Sabi Juarez, a woman who has been kind enough to offer you her couch and who fed you a piece of Chicken Teriyaki with her chopsticks earlier.

TESTING FOR LICE

If you're a nurse at an elementary school and you hear from one of the teachers that a louse was spotted on a desk in the first-grade classroom just a few minutes ago, you must test everyone for lice. This is best done with rubber gloves and chopsticks. You must summon all the first-graders and have them form a line outside of your office. Then you must check their scalps, one by one, using your chopsticks to lift their hair and look beneath it. You will find some children more cooperative than others. Some will be angry. Some will protest at the sight of you with your rubber gloves and chopsticks. Others, the kids who never get a tender touch from their parents or from anyone else, will seem to enjoy the touch of your chopsticks. I remember closing my eyes and feeling her chopsticks in my hair. I remember the feeling was ecstasy—the chopsticks, her hand keeping me from swaying, her breath on my neck, the darkness because my eyes were closed and I had entered a state of deep relaxation—and then the sound of her voice telling me to go on, move it. I remember walking around to the back of the line.

TAKING GIFTS

It's great to get gifts sometimes, but other times it can be not so great. By taking a gift from the wrong people you can find yourself in their debt. This means they can ask you to do stuff you don't want to do and you'll feel like you have to do it. Taking gifts from strangers, including the gift of hospitality, is always a gamble. All you can do is hope that the gift-giver doesn't ask for repayment that you can't offer. If your uncle gives you a radio, and if you know that your uncle is basically a good person, then you can take the radio and use it in your treehouse without worrying that he'll come by asking you to clean the gutters of the mansion. If a little boy you don't know offers you his milk carton and the two of you are in the cafeteria at a bunkhouse for boys and girls who are wards of the state, it should occur to you that this milk-carton gift is meant as payment for your protecting him. If a woman you just met in a parking lot offers you her couch to sleep on and takeout Chinese food for dinner once you get there, and on top of it she lights a joint in the living room while you're watching telenovelas, it might occur to you that she'll want more than for you to run chopsticks through her hair.

TEMPTATION

For the toy dog, there is no temptation as strong as the sardine being dangled above its head. It must battle its wild-dog genes with the good manners it has been taught over the years, and it will wait, fixated on the sardine, until its master says, "Goo-boy take it." Or this: You're in a financial crisis. You're out of money. Your mansion has a huge insurance package covering fire damage—all you have to do is build a fire inside and cash in. Or: You're living beneath a bridge over a river. You dream of floating down the river but you're not sure how, then one day a bunch of barrels washes ashore from some place upriver where they're manufacturing a substance that goes in those barrels. When you fortuitously see the pile of barrels (see MEETING FORTUITOUSLY) floating in an eddy of water by the banks below your bridge, you'll be

tempted to lash them into a raft. All jumps are in some
way tempting. All voids beckon. When you look out the
window of your treehouse at the ground far below you, the
idea of falling that far is tempting because you've never felt
what it feels like to fall that far. If the events of the past
few days have run you down, let's just say, as an example,
that your raft was obliterated, you were arrested, and you
learned that your father had committed suicide, your willpower will be sapped and temptations that appear will
overpower you. If you're alone in a house with a woman
you hardly know, a woman who was the age you are now
on the day you were born, and this woman makes it clear
that she would like it if you took her clothes off, how
tempted you feel to take her clothes off will depend on the
answers to a number of questions. Is she nice? Does her
house feel comfortable? Does she seem like a Daddy in a
bad way, or does she just seem lonely because her husband
recently left her to be with a woman he met at his work?
When Sabi parts the beaded curtain between the living
room and her bedroom and she's wearing a nightgown,
how do you feel? Do you want to know what it feels like
to have sex?

TOKYO SONATAS
Amazing, beautiful compositions for the synthesizer and
marimba produced in the 1970s by a group of scientists

and artists in Tokyo, Japan, the TOKYO SONATAS are only available on a vinyl record I haven't been able to find anywhere except in a crate in Sabi Juarez's living room. Genius is random, shows up like a submarine, and disappears, is what Sabi said. Genius hit the Tokyo people hard in 1974. I'll never forget hearing the beautiful sounds of the TOKYO SONATAS at Sabi's house. I use the word BEAUTIFUL for the TOKYO SONATAS, and the word BEAUTIFUL has, so far, appeared six times in this key, but I have never properly defined it. I have never understood what the word beautiful means, but it's something like this: everything you know, all the names of things, they're coming to a point. In the middle of the night, before you and Sabi take the dog for a moonlight walk, she has you hold him while she tenderly slips his two back legs, and then his two front legs, through the holes in a thin red sweater. She says, "Beautiful," and you put the dog down.

TENDERNESS

See the woman at the park holding a baby, bouncing the baby lightly in her arms? That's tenderness. You and your pal Ned are running through the woods and Ned falls and skins his knee on a rock. He limps the rest of the way to the treehouse. He's trying not to cry and blood is running down his leg. After you get the Band-Aids from the treehouse wound kit and put one on his knee for him, you must pat down the Band-Aid with tenderness. If you wake up in a bed with a woman, treat her tenderly, and she will do the same for you. Don't leave early in the morning without saying goodbye, especially if the night before she tenderly held you in her arms as you told her all about your life. She listened. That was tender of her. Still, it's tempting to sneak away. The sunlight of crepuscular dawn, when it touches your sunburned face, is tender.

TOILETRY BAG
Bag that holds the things you normally use in bathrooms. Toiletry bags are small, made of shiny plastic fabric, and covered in designs. Toiletry bags are used when you're on the road so that everything is in one place when you stop at a bathroom. If all you have is a toothbrush, you don't need a toiletry bag. If you're floating down a river on a raft, the best place for your toothbrush is on a string around your neck so you can find it in the dark and it doesn't get lost overboard. If a woman has a toiletry bag in her hand, car keys in her other, a backpack full of clothes slung over one arm and a toy dog in a red leather bag slung over the other—let's say you're sitting in her kitchen eating a bowl of cereal when she comes in with her bags and her car keys—you can be sure she's planning to go somewhere, and soon, and that she intends to take you with her.

TENSE

A toy dog meeting two full-grown German shepherds it has never met before: the toy dog will be tense. Tense is the opposite of relaxed. Tense can be a state of mind, but it can also have to do with the space of time. A TENSE moment, written in the PAST TENSE, might be this: The warden of the bunkhouse, Wilson Carmichael, held in his hands a little snapping turtle that he'd pulled from the sheets of the bunk belonging to a boy named Ernesto, and as the little turtle snapped the air, hissed, and flailed its webbed feet, Wilson Carmichael looked around at the gathering of orphans and said, "Who put this in Ernesto's bed?" A tense moment, in the present tense, present because it's not yet a memory when you say it: "I can't go on a road trip with you right now, Sabi, I'm sorry," and when you say it she's standing there with her floral toiletry bag and her backpack of clothes and her car keys and her toy Chihuahua and a map of the Southwestern states she had spread out on the table earlier—"deserts, Anasazi pueblos, every kind of Indian artifact, slickrock canyons, I know you'll love it," she said. A tense moment, begun with a sentence in future tense: "I will get on that Greyhound bus after all, take it back to where I came from, tie up some loose ends, and get on with my life."

TYING UP LOOSE ENDS

Picture an old net lying in a patch of weeds beside an old shack on the banks of a river. Imagine it's the kind of net that has weights woven into it, the kind of net you throw into a body of water by twisting at the hips and flinging it like a big disc, the kind of net that, when thrown like this and then pulled back ashore, is meant to come up filled with fish. Imagine spreading out this old net, untangling its many strange tangles (you'll need a flat, quiet, weed-free place to do this, and you'll need plenty of time to work). Imagine the old net lying flat on a driveway. Imagine that this net has a number of large holes, places where mice ate their way through it or where fish burst through, holes from where the net got caught on a submerged log sunk deep in the mud. Then imagine you have a spool of new line, a sharp knife, and the whole day ahead of you. Imagine that each little square of this net is a memory in your head, a memory of a time something happened, or a memory of something you heard somebody say once. When you think about the sequence of things that happened to bring you where you are today, it's like you're looking at a hopelessly tangled, useless net. Let's say you're sitting at a bus stop wondering what the hell you're doing. WHAT AM I DOING?— that's an unanswerable question and to ask it of yourself can make you feel like you're looking at a tangled net on the banks of a river teeming with fish. The only thing to do, in that moment, is to work with your line and your knife, square by square, repairing the mesh of your net. When at last all the holes are gone, it's time to tie up the loose ends, the places near the edge of the net close to where the weights are. Once this is done, all you have to do is learn how to cast.

TYPEWRITER
A machine that writes type, used by writers to make documents that look official. You may be the greatest writer of all time but until you have a typewriter your work will not be taken seriously.

Sabi, when I told her I wasn't going to go along on her tour of the Southwest, when I told her that she had her important business and I had mine and we both needed to go forth alone, took it pretty well. "At least let me take you to the bus stop," she said, and I said, "of course," and before we got in her car she put a boxy leather case on the kitchen table, a case with a shiny metal lock and a rigid frame, and she told me to open it. Inside the case was a typewriter. She showed me how to load the paper in the top and twist the feeder until the paper came back up, showed me how to return the paper to the start of a new line.

ULTRAMARINE

The bluest shade of blue. Bluer than this and you're going into purple. Less blue and you're headed to gray, and from there you could be heading anywhere. The roofs of stucco buildings in Greece are ultramarine. In crepuscular light look up, find the first star to appear in the night—it will be in a sky that is still blue, a darkening patch of daytime sky, that's where you'll glimpse ultramarine. The best place to find ultramarine is through the tall, gently vibrating glass windows of a Greyhound bus in late summer.

USHERED IN

When somebody puts his hand on your back, pushes you gently through a door, and closes it behind you. The only way I can come up with a reason for my father's suicide is if I make one up using what I know about myself. The reason will come from my genes: my father waded into that water because not even his photographs could show people the world as he saw it, and because he missed my mother, and because he realized that the one thing he really knew how to do couldn't help him do what he wanted to do. At that point he decided that death would be better for him than life. When he made the decision, he also decided something for me. He decided his being dead would be better for me than his being alive. I will honor his wishes and believe he was right. I will have him silently standing behind a closed door that's somewhere behind me.

ULULATE

Sounds something like an OPERATIC FALSETTO but is not, to ululate is to make high-pitched, strange noises with your throat and lungs. People ululate when they're sad about something. Women from the Middle East are the most famous ululators though they can't be the only ones. If you're watching the news on a TV in a Greyhound station and a reporter is giving a live dispatch from a town in the Middle East that was bombed to rubble a day earlier, and behind the reporter are the people whose homes were destroyed, and they start to ululate, all of a sudden you'll want to cry because although your luck isn't the best, really, you would, if you could, give some of your luck to the ululators. All the things you've clung to might seem senseless in the face of what's on the television. You'll realize that nothing you could say is as important as what's being said by the brokenhearted mother on the screen. You may think it's a coincidence that ULULATE starts with a U and that you've learned its meaning at a time when you're feeling so close to Z—and then, outside, in the park across from the bus stop, you see a man atop a unicycle juggling apples for a group of children. When you're on a bus that's leaving the station and you're waving goodbye to a newfound friend who just dropped you off, you may, in your mind, be ululating.

UNDERRIPE FRUIT
Fruit that's not ready to eat yet but that in some situations you must eat anyway. Let's say you were in a rush to get on a bus, that the doors of the bus were about to close and you needed to get on that bus because you needed to go where that bus was going but your stomach was grumbling and all you had was a little bag of clothes, a toothbrush, a camera, and a typewriter, let's say that at that point you spot a withered old apple tree behind a bench where some old men are awaiting a bus of their own, and you dash over to the tree, leaving your things on a seat by the window in the bus whose doors are about to close, and, though the driver says, "We're leaving now," you blow past him and run flat-out to the tree, snatch three apples and run back, up the steps of the bus and through the door, which snaps shut behind you. You then sit down and bite into the first of your apples, but your teeth barely sink through the skin and the apple meat breaks off like a tiny coin in your mouth, and the underripe taste sends shocks of pain to the gland beneath your left ear.

ULTRA POSSE NEMO OBLIGATUR

This is Latin for the idea that you can't be expected to do more than you are physically or emotionally capable of doing. It's a legal term, and legal terms are written in Latin because the judges and lawyers want to keep people who aren't judges and lawyers out of their conversations. If the law were in English, a judge would spend too much time explaining what he means to the people in court and not enough time judging them. The good news is that you can get to his level if you know what to do. First, go to the library and find the section with law books. These books will be fat and heavy, will all look the same, and there won't be a lot of people browsing through them. Pick one out, flip to the back, find the Latin words with English translations, and spend some time trying to see if you can apply these words to hypothetical court cases against people you've met over the course of your life. Also memorize a few phrases that seem general enough that they might come in handy in the courtroom one day. ULTRA POSSE NEMO OBLIGATUR, for example, is a saying that could work in a number of situations. If you're trying to explain to El Hondero why you forgive him for walking out on you, for going solo on his wild goose chase for mica in Ohio, and you want to explain it to him in a way that makes it seem official and not too emotional—if you don't want to just say "I missed you and I was mad at you but I'm back now, let's be friends"—you could just say "Hey, ultra posse nemo obligatur, man" and give him a high five, and that'll make everything better. If your plan is to show up in court and try to convince a judge that he should go easy on your uncle, you'd better have some Latin in your back pocket so that you can sound official. Even better—go to the courthouse in a suit and a tie with a recent haircut and a letter you typed up on a typewriter and addressed to the judge. A judge likes having a letter hand-delivered to her when she's alone in her chambers, drinking a cup of coffee and looking over a case, especially if the letter is delivered to her by a reformed young ward of the state.

UNORTHODOX METHODS
There is a method to driving a bus full of passengers. If the bus driver follows the standard method of driving a bus, he will most likely get the bus from A to Z without calamity. His method will involve staying in one lane, not exceeding the speed limit, and restricting swerves. Not all bus drivers drive according to this tried-and-true method. Some drivers employ unorthodox methods. Some drivers attempt to drive while sleeping, while shouting angrily on a cell phone, and while eating enormous sandwiches that cause condiment spill-outs on driver uniforms, curses on the part of the driver, and spastic corrections of the bus's direction. To

write a story in alphabetical order is unorthodox, but if you're trying to tell a lot of stories all at once and you're trying to tell them for a lot of different reasons, you must resort to unorthodox methods.

UNEVENTFUL

If someone says, "How was your trip?" and you say, "It was uneventful," you mean to say that your trip went smoothly, that it did not include unpredictable events which forced you to change plans while on the run. A ride on a bus can be uneventful when in fact it was full of tiny events that weren't really worth remembering but at the time were events of note. On my eventful journey down the river on my raft made of barrels I was faced with roiling eddies, huge, submerged trees, sudden, mid-river waterfalls that would appear and disappear again in moments, enormous fish, a burning sun, mystical visions, and a shipwreck. On my uneventful bus trip back to where I'd come from I was faced with a talkative office clerk who'd been visiting an old friend from college, a woman who ate two whole fried chickens, who sported huge fake nails which she sucked clean again and again, who nearly touched me with those nails as she made her way down the bus aisle toward the bathroom. I also experienced several strange naps filled with bizarre dreams from which I woke sweating and disoriented, and that was about it. After I'd gotten off the bus, walked a mile to the old iron bridge, climbed up to El Hondero's little apartment and found him sitting in his chair poring over yet another map of yet another wilderness, and after he'd given me a peanut-butter sandwich, sat me down in a chair, and asked me how my trip had gone, first I told him about the events going down there, of all that had happened in the town by the river, and then I told him the trip back had been uneventful.

UNCERTAINTY

It is for certain that everything is, ultimately, uncertain. A sentence that begins IT IS could always be continued with the word UNCERTAIN, and this would in any context certainly be true. It has a bunch of people inside and it is driving north on a road, and among the people inside of it is a woman who has eaten two fried chickens and who is now on her way to the tiny bathroom in the rear of it. Is it a bus? Yes. Though it is not certainly a bus. It could be a very long, specialized limousine. The purpose of adding an entry entitled UNCERTAINTY is to resolve uncertainties that have, by this time, built up as a result of my private language. It is certain that I was traveling north on a bus when I saw a woman eat two fried chickens in quick succession, though she may have eaten more than two chickens—I say two fried chickens though

I am certain that the parts she ate would not, if you found and reassembled them, result in two whole chickens—and it is true that I became certain, after seeing her go into the bathroom, that I would not go in there for some uncertain but long amount of time once she'd come out. Of what else was I, at that time, certain? I was certain that I would, in a few hours, get off the bus, orient myself, and then set off in the direction of the bridge over the river onto which I had launched my raft of barrels. I was uncertain that I would make it to the bridge without being confronted by some new, unforeseen obstacle. An enormous ship could long ago have destroyed the bridge while trying to pass beneath it. Would I be run over by a pickup truck belonging to park maintenance workers on an off-road joyride as I passed through a city park en route to the old bridge? Unlikely, but also uncertain. I'd recently seen a man pop out his own eye and use it as fishing tackle (see SAYNKER), which was one of many things I'd recently seen that had taught me about the hazards of expectation (see EXPECTATION). Would there be anything left of the old treehouse I'd built in the sycamore that one year it rained really hard and my uncle's basement flooded? That, too, was uncertain, and the thought that I might be able to resolve the uncertainty of the existence of treehouse ruins was enticing . . . though I put the possibility out of my mind for the moment because it is best to tie up your loose ends one by one.

UNNAMING

In theory, this would be to take a name away from something that has been named. If you can figure out how to unname something without renaming it, you might have discovered time travel. A dog that belongs to a hermit and has never seen anyone but the hermit will, when the hermit dies and the dog becomes wild, still keep his name, even if nobody else knows it.

VANITY

A word for something that happens when you look at yourself in the mirror. Vanity is the obsession with one's image, an obsession that appears in a mirror when you think no one else is looking. I remember the subtle shift in El Hondero's face whenever he caught sight of it in a mirror. He would stop, bring his lips together, and do something like a frown with his mouth, though it was not really a frown, it was something else. The face he made in the mirror was a private expression, an expression he thought was secret, and watching it made me think of the privacy you get when you put your head in a body of water—the silence, the slowing of time, the loneliness of divers . . . I remember seeing my uncle catch himself in a mirror once, the mirror in the living room. He didn't know I was watching him. He was crossing the room when he caught sight of himself in the mirror. He stopped in front of the mirror and a look of horror came over his face. He brought his hand to his mouth, as if gasping, then began to rub his skin like he was testing how it felt. I don't know if there's a subtle face I make when I look in the mirror. Am I vain? Did I ever look into the muddy surface of the river, which was sometimes a brown mirror, and try to pick out my eyes and nose and mouth as shifting shades of brown? Did I make faces at myself for an hour in the water one particularly boring day? Can you ever shake your vanity? Soon after I was back from my journey down the river I spent an entire hour at a thrift shop, trying on used suits and looking at myself in the mirror before riding the bus to Isabella's apartment. I needed the suit for the judge, not for Isabella, who had finished exploring her inner self in Mexico City, but about that—the suit not being just a little bit for Isabella as well—I am uncertain. Right before we left to go see my uncle in prison, Isabella made her mirror-face in a mirror. She was standing in the dim hallway of her apartment. El Hondero was paging through a book on her coffee table, and I was standing there in her living room with my arms crossed when I saw her, looking at herself in the mirror, making a face I hadn't seen before. Then she carefully put on a layer of red lipstick, smacked her lips once, and saw me in the mirror, watching her looking at herself in the mirror. We made eye contact. My stomach dropped out. She stared at me for several seconds. I don't know what she was trying to say by staring at me like she did. Then she dropped her lipstick in her purse, snapped it shut, came into the living room, and we left.

VISUAL AID
I once had a photograph my father took of himself. It wasn't a vain photograph, at least not in the usual way. In the photograph he was outside the bus we lived in and it was windy so his hair was being blown to the side. I remember he looked a lot like my uncle, and he was looking into the camera like my uncle looked into the mirror.

VORTEX
Swirling void, like an eddy, which sucks things into its center. A vortex can appear in all kinds of places. The only requirements for a vortex are the following:

1. It must be sucking things into it. Things can include you, a bunch of floating sticks, or even just your mind. I once saw a vortex and felt it suck my mind in. It was a cool, clear night. I was on my belly, lying on an old iron bridge, looking between its rusty iron beams at the surface of the water where the water was still, having pooled up on the

bank, where it was reflecting the stars and the shadow of the iron bridge and the shape of my head looking into the water.

2. The vortex, to be a vortex, must remain a vortex over time. If, for instance, you look through the iron beams of a bridge at a spot where river water is pooled up on the riverbank and you behold a vortex there, you must be able to return to that spot where you saw the vortex before, lie down on the beams, and see it again.

3. A vortex, like a nexus, can be where things come together. A place can be a vortex, and so can a person.

VULNERABLE

The white flesh at the base of a turtle's neck, when it sticks its head from its shell, is vulnerable. Your skin, when it isn't covered in fabric and you're floating down a river in the blinding heat of day, is vulnerable to the sun. By night, to the mosquitoes. When someone shows you he's vulnerable, he's trusting you not to attack him. When you see that he is vulnerable, and he knows you can see it, you and he will become more deeply connected. For example, I once thought of El Hondero as something like a god. Then he showed me the scars his father had given him as a child. He lifted his shirt and showed me the scars on his back on that afternoon when I returned to the bridge. He showed me his scars and let me feel them with my fingers.

WEARY
When you feel you can't go on, but you must. El Hondero put his hand on my shoulder and said, "My boy, you are weary. Let me help you go on." It is easier not to be weary in company than it is when you're alone. Look at the guys who shovel gravel all day. If you've ever shoveled gravel, you know how terrible it is. No shovel is the proper shovel for gravel. Shovel gravel alone, you quickly become weary. Shovel gravel with people, take breaks with them, leaning up against the gravel truck, you're less weary. When you say, "Goddamn it's hot," and another gravel shoveler replies, "Goddamn it's hot," it somehow cools the air down.

WINE GARB
Good wine is properly had by sipping from a wineglass while you are wearing a suit. Good wine is for special occasions, like when you're reunited with your cousin, and it helps you talk to people if you're nervous and aren't sure what to say. Wine is better than the beer that comes in big glass bottles because wine is fine even if it's warm, and because El Hondero and Isabella bonded over a

particular bottle of wine that, evidently, they had both had before, although I had my doubts as to whether or not El Hondero was telling the truth about having had this particular bottle of wine, same as I had my doubts as to whether or not Isabella was truly a fan of the Dom Perrota Fresh-Leaf Cigarillos that El Hondero always carried in the front pocket of his trench coat. It is best for you to leave and go find a park to hang out in if your cousin and your best friend are having a heated discussion about Bolivia, drinking wine, and laughing at things that aren't funny—especially if outside it's nearing dusk and there's a bench you know in the park and you've been meaning to write someone a letter.

WISHING UPON STARS

It is written in a famous song that if you wish upon a falling star your wish will come true. This is not the case. You make your own wishes come true, and besides that it's all luck. Maybe if you wish upon a star and believe that your wish will come true you will find whatever it takes to keep waiting for long enough and then, eventually, because you've been patient, luck will come your way and help you out. It won't really be the star that helped you, but in the end it won't matter if you tell yourself it was. Luck is luck. Maybe there's more to it than that. Maybe it is the stars. Maybe I accidentally wished upon

one once. Maybe I wished upon one and it traveled mil-
lions of light-years to come and help me. Maybe it was
what guided Sabi Juarez my way, or maybe it was why El
Hondero stopped me from getting into the water beneath
the bridge that one night.

WONDER

The explorer, hacking his way through the jungle, hears
his machete ping against rock and finds an enormous
granite statue swallowed up in the vines. He falls to his
knees before this statue, joyful and in awe: this is wonder.
Floating slowly down a river at night beneath a starry sky
and a crescent moon, the hills dark curves moving
against the lighter darkness of deep space, the seahorse
nebula, all the sounds of animals and insects coming
from those hills, a thin swarm of lightning bugs flashing
over the soggy bottomlands at the feet of the hills: this
is wonder.

WOUNDS, THE HEALING AND REOPENING OF

A wound is a physical injury that doesn't necessarily kill
you. A broken tailbone sustained after falling out of a
treehouse can be classified as a wound, as can rope burn
or a dog bite. Wounds can also be emotional. Your heart
can be wounded and it can feel like it's going to kill you.
Imagine you find out your friend has changed the

treehouse password and won't give you the new one. That's going to wound you emotionally, and you may want to wound your friend in return. But it's best just to leave, wait, and let your wound heal. Imagine your guardian—the person on whom you rely for food and shelter, the source of your basic living requirements— imagine he burns down the house you live in, gets put in jail for arson, and becomes completely unable to help you in any way. You will be wounded. This wound will take a long time to heal and will maybe never finish healing. If you're sitting in a car with El Hondero and Isabella, and the car is parked outside a big, ugly building with barbed wire around it and a sign that says SCHLITZ CENTER FOR REFORMING ADULTS, and you know that inside the building is your uncle—your cousin's father, the guy who hurt you both so deeply—you'll need to decide whether or not to run the risk of seeing him. Seeing him could deepen the wound he made, or it could heal you. If you finally decide to go in, you should go through the jailhouse gate alone.

WITNESS

In a court trial, the judge hears a story. Based on this story, he decides what to do with the main characters. The main characters try to make the judge do what they want him to do by telling their sides of the story. When a character tells a story in court, he becomes known as a witness. If you are going to be a witness, you will want to have witnessed something related to the story that the judge is hearing, preferably something big, something meaningful, something that the judge will be moved by emotionally (see OVERBOARD, GOING). Your story must also be believable. You will want to walk into the court with facts. You will want the judge, and everyone else in the court, to know exactly what you mean when you speak your language.

WITHDRAWAL OF CHARGES

This is when you've done something illegal and go to court as a defendant and stand trial before the judge, and then all of a sudden the plaintiffs stand up and yell WE WITHDRAW THE CHARGES. In movies, this happens because a star witness shows up out of the blue and is able to make the plaintiffs change their minds by telling an amazing story—a story that shows you didn't really do the illegal thing that everyone says you did—and then the charges are withdrawn, which means you can go free. This is a thing that only happens in movies. This is a thing that does not happen if you burn down your own house in order to collect insurance money and you've admitted it. If you're charged with arson and insurance fraud, nobody stands up and says WE WITHDRAW THE

CHARGES, no matter how moving or amazing a story the star witness, who has shown up out of the blue, tells. The mansion was worth money, and money is worth more than everything to some people.

WORK-RELEASE PROGRAM

But they can let him go on a work-release program. The judge can let him leave jail for a day here, a day there—first to shovel gravel, and then the judge can decide to loan him out more permanently so that he can help you build a special library at a bunkhouse for wards of the state. You will have proposed the library in a document addressed to the judge and to Wilson Carmichael. Your uncle is an excellent candidate for the position of bunkhouse librarian because he has experience. In his mansion he once kept a vast trove of reference materials that he single-handedly kept meticulously organized, although they were, unfortunately, destroyed in the blaze. He is also an excellent candidate because the men on the gravel team will, once they've seen him shovel, vouch for his work ethic. Finally, your uncle can bugle the reveille at the bunkhouse every morning. If your uncle is good at all these things, which he will be, the judge might let him go free a little early, and you will have a place to live again.

XYLOPHONE, HOMEMADE

Of all the tone-producing percussion instruments, a xylophone is the easiest to make at home. All you need to do is find chunks of flat metal, attach them to a hollow wooden box, and bang on them with sticks or mallets or even just your knuckles. Different metal pieces produce different sounds, and the wooden box that the bars are sitting on amplifies the sounds they make when you hit them with mallets. When I at last got the chance to see my uncle in the Schlitz Center, I beheld a homemade xylophone. A guard led me into the common area of the prison. Isabella and El Hondero were waiting in the car outside. In the common area I saw him at a little table by a barred window, looking outside at the thunderclouds that were rising up in the distance. I guess he didn't get many chances to look out windows in prison, because he was so fixated on those clouds that he didn't notice me enter or respond when the guard yelled his name. Around us, at other little tables, other inmates were meeting with their families. I was too nervous to go over to my uncle at first. I stood there, frozen at the door, thinking all of a sudden that I didn't want to be there, that I didn't want to meet him. Then I heard the sound of a mallet hitting a homemade xylophone over and over, someone playing out the notes of a song. I found the source: over in the corner, at a table, an old man in jail clothes sat across from a young man my age. Between them on the table was the xylophone, which the old man had made himself and was hitting with his mallets. It was obvious that this old man had worked for many hours on the instrument and on perfecting the song, and that he'd done it all in preparation for this moment. I thought about my uncle's bugle. I pictured it buried in the ashes of his mansion. That's when I walked over to my uncle, who was still lost and looking out at that sky, and sat down across from him.

YONDER, THE WILD BLUE

What my uncle was looking at out the window when I sat down across from him at the little table in the jailhouse visiting room. The wild blue yonder is where I was headed when I launched my raft. The wild blue yonder is where characters go at the ends of books. We say you've gone into the wild blue yonder when you disappear over the horizon and we don't know exactly where you're heading. We do know that wherever it is, it's over that horizon in the yonder, which, if I'm watching you pass into it, is blue, and it looks like you're walking into the sky.

I CANNOT SAY HOW MUCH YOU HELPED ME:

Padgett Powell, the Flamingo Prince, and Johnny Hamm. Also Holly Pratt, David Reed, and MFA@FLA '17 and '18, but especially Trevor Crown, Arthur Thuot, and Glen Lindquist. Thank you Sharon Killfoyle, Joe Dames, Paul Weber, Emily Wright, Lee Malis, Patricia Basurto, Jill Ciment, Amy Hempel, Geoff Demitz, and Neal Thompson. Thank you to the Trimarcos, and thank you to the Reeds in Orangeburg. Thank you to my agent Markus Hoffmann, and such deep gratitude to everyone at Tin House: Masie Cochran, Nanci McCloskey, Sabrina Wise, and Diane Chonette.

ELLIOT REED received his MFA from the
University of Florida in Gainesville and currently lives
in Spokane, Washington.